TEXAS VENGEANCE

Luther Bastian's younger brother was murdered by outlaws. Now Bastian is a bounty hunter who comes to kill — unable to be reasoned with, persuaded or bribed. So when a gang of lawless men brutally slay a Texas Ranger, Captain Mallory knows just the man to call on. But during the pursuit, Bastian is befriended by a young woman and a small boy. Can they change his view on the world, and put an end to his quest for vengeance?

Books by Ralph Hayes
in the Linford Western Library:

THE TOMBSTONE VENDETTA
FORT REVENGE
THE LAST BUFFALO

RALPH HAYES

TEXAS VENGEANCE

Complete and Unabridged

LINFORD
Leicester

First published in Great Britain in 2014 by
Robert Hale Limited
London

First Linford Edition
published 2016
by arrangement with
Robert Hale
an imprint of
The Crowood Press
Wiltshire

A catalogue record for this book is available
from the British Library.

ISBN 978–1–4448–3078–1

Published by
F. A. Thorpe (Publishing)
Anstey, Leicestershire

Set by Words & Graphics Ltd.
Anstey, Leicestershire
Printed and bound in Great Britain by
T. J. International Ltd., Padstow, Cornwall

This book is printed on acid-free paper

For Donna, who tells her
charismatic stories on canvas

1

Ethan Purvis looked up from a pile of documents on his long oak desk and frowned at the gangly-looking young man who had just entered his office holding two slips of paper in his hand. Trailing behind him a couple of paces, sober-faced, was a ten-year-old boy.

'Got a couple interesting wires for you this morning, Mayor,' the thin fellow announced, walking over and laying the scraps of paper down in front of Purvis. 'They're both from the sheriff down at Stinking Creek. One come just after the other. He thinks we might be in for some trouble right soon. Oh. This here is the Spencer kid.'

'What?' Purvis said distractedly, glancing at the boy. The mayor had gray in his hair and a pot belly that was hidden by the desk.

The blondish youngster with a

1

scattering of freckles across his face came up beside the fellow from the telegraph office. His manner was glum.

'Jonah Spencer, Mr Mayor. You sent for me.'

Purvis stared at him blankly for a moment. 'Oh. Yes. Take a seat over there, boy. I want to talk with you.'

Jonah hesitated, then walked over to a straight-backed chair sat against an end wall and seated himself gingerly on it. He was a good-looking boy with dark-blue eyes and a strong chin. He folded his hands on his knees.

Mayor Purvis picked up the hand-printed messages and read them in order of their receipt. His face fell into straight lines and he muttered an obscenity.

As if the messages required clarification, the telegraph operator began a summary. 'The Gabriel gang is in Stinking Creek,' he said a bit breathlessly. 'The sheriff there is keeping his distance, but he heard they might be heading this way.' He watched Purvis's face. 'He knows we got no law here now.'

'I can read your scribbling, Foley.'

'What do you plan to do, Mayor? We're kind of defenseless here. You thought we could get along without a sheriff when old Silas quit. And now look.'

Purvis cast a brittle look his way. 'Nobody wanted the job, Foley. Would you like to apply for it?'

Foley grinned awkwardly. 'Why, I got me a job, Mayor. I'm just thinking. Gabriel's got some hardcases riding with him. That Cuckoo Bobo's got bats in his belfry. Whenever he shoots a man, or the gang does, he takes himself a trophy.'

'A what?'

'He takes a souvenir off the corpse, something that belonged to the dead man. He keeps it all in a cigar box. And that Cottonwood Eddie sold a Comanche head to a traveling medicine show.'

Purvis shook his head to stop him, gesturing toward a raptly attentive Jonah.

'Oh. Yeah. Did you see the second wire? About the Cheyenne Kid?'

'Yes, Foley. The one that's terrorized

the Staked Plains for three years running, and is now raising hell right here in Greer County, at Sloan's Crossroads. But that's farther south than Stinking Creek. It was good of the sheriff to alert us, though.'

'If he joined up with Gabriel, that gang would be unstoppable,' Foley suggested in a hushed tone.

'No gang is unstoppable,' Purvis said quietly, wondering if he believed it.

'The Texas Rangers can stop them,' Jonah said from across the room.

Purvis smiled a tired smile. 'Son, we haven't seen a Ranger in Medicine Bend in a coon's age. They're spread out pretty thin nowadays, and they're needed more around places like Abilene and Dallas. And the US marshals are busy in the Territory.'

'There was a Ranger up north of here on the border a while back,' Foley said. 'Maybe his superiors would order him here, if Gabriel shows up here to give us trouble.'

'That's Eli St Clair you heard about,'

Purvis told him. 'He used to come through here when I first took office. But he won't be sent here. The Rangers HQ at Austin probably doesn't even know Gabriel is in this area yet. Send a wire off to Sheriff Provost, Foley. Thank him for the warnings. Then forget it, I'm sure we'll be all right.'

Foley nodded. 'If you say so.' Then he turned and left.

Purvis sat there for a long moment, then looked over at Jonah. 'I wish you didn't have to hear all that, boy. Come over here to my desk.'

Jonah got up and walked slowly to another chair at the desk, and sat heavily on it.

'I'm sorry to hear about your grandfather, Jonah.'

Jonah feigned nonchalance. 'I reckon old folks die. That's the way it is.'

'When is the funeral?'

'In a couple days, I guess.'

Purvis studied the boy's face, trying to get the telegraph messages out of his head. 'You realize you can't live out at that cabin alone, don't you?'

'It's my home,' Jonah said. 'It was our home.'

'I know. I understand your parents were taken off by that diphtheria epidemic that swept through here a few years back. Was Ed your only living relative?'

Jonah sighed. 'Gramps said I got an aunt. Over in the Territory. A place called Kiowa Junction. Her name is Maggie. Maggie Spencer.'

Purvis nodded. 'Well, we may have to send you to her. I can get in touch by wire. The trouble is, there's no stage line going that way from here. I'll have to figure that out. In the meantime, there's a cot out back in our stable. You can sleep there, and eat meals with the missus and me if you behave yourself. We'll feed you till you're gone.'

Jonah heard the reluctance in his voice. 'I can take care of myself.'

Purvis grunted. 'Sure you can. Just like this town can take care of itself. You just do what I tell you, boy. Feeding you might be the least of my problems soon.

6

Now you go tell the missus to get you some bedding for that cot. I'll talk to you later.'

'I'm sure the Rangers will take care of that gang, Mr Mayor,' Jonah said reassuringly. 'They always get their man.'

Purvis let another smile cross his lined face. 'I heard that myself, boy,' he replied quietly.

★   ★   ★

It was just the next day when, at Stinking Creek, the Gabriel gang tired of drinking and gambling at the local saloon, and Simon Gabriel made the decision that would have made Ethan Purvis's face go pale. He decided to move on north and east, with the idea of heading back into Indian Territory from which they had come and where most of them had earned their ugly reputations. Gabriel had hoped for a few bank and stage robberies in Texas but nothing had enticed him. On their way back to the Territory they would

7

pass through Medicine Bend.

Gabriel and his cohorts rode out at just after noon that day. There were Cuckoo Bobo and Cottonwood Eddie; a Mexican, Pedro Rueda; a fancy Dan named Sweet Daddy; and a sharp-shooting woman called Big Thelma. All killers. And all looking for trouble.

Later that day, in Sloan's Crossroads, the Cheyenne Kid had also gotten bored with his surroundings. The village con-sisted only of two dozen residences, a stage depot with rented rooms on the second floor, a store and a saloon. The Kid had drunk his fill at the Lost Dogie saloon without paying a three-cent nickel for it, shot up some advertising signs outside the small general store, and raped a young widow in her home on the previous, moonless night. And since there was no law in the Crossroads, nobody had made the effort to report the crime to authorities.

Now, in early evening at the stage depot where the Kid ate and slept during his brief stay, he had gotten word about the Gabriel gang being near by, and that they were headed for Medicine Bend. The Kid had heard of Gabriel, and had imagined a profitable partnership with him. The thought occurred to him that he might ride north the following day to Medicine Bend and seek out Gabriel to talk about joining him there.

That would have been the second bit of news unwelcome to Mayor Purvis.

But at just before sunset there was a development that added another factor into the plans of the Kid. A stranger rode into town.

The few citizens who saw him ride past them down to the Lost Dogie stopped and stared hard. He rode a glossy black stallion with a white star on its forehead, and the rider himself was dressed all in black. He was a tall man, with dark hair and eyes, wearing a black Stetson, a black riding-coat over a dark, formal suit, and black boots with heavy silver spurs. At his throat was a black lariat tie over the only relief from ebony: a plain white shirt. His name was Luther Bastian, but because of his clergy-looking attire, together with the Christian name of Luther, he was also refered to as the Preacher by those who had encountered him and lived to report the fact. He was a bounty hunter, despised by outlaws and lawmen alike, and even by others who practiced the same profession.

The difference between Bastian and the few other men of his trade in the region was that Bastian pursued only men wanted dead or alive, and with substantial rewards on their heads. Also, he had never brought an outlaw in alive. He was regarded by the law as a man who murdered for money.

Bastian dismounted fluidly at the hitching rail outside the saloon, wrapped the mount's reins over the rail there, and then removed the riding-coat. His face was well-formed, but long and angular. His eyes were unnervingly piercing, and his face was usually expressionless. He now put his hand on the horse's muzzle, and the animal guffered quietly at the touch. A rider came down the street and paused to study him for a moment, taking note of the two saddle scabbards on the stallion's flanks, holding a Winchester 1866 lever-action rifle, and a Remington eight-gauge, double-barreled shotgun.

'Excuse me, mister. You wouldn't be the law, would you?'

Bastian turned to face him, and the rider saw the sawed-off Colt Peacemaker .44 that lay across Bastian's belly in a custom, break-open holster. What he could not see was the Meriden five-shot pocket revolver in a small shoulder holster under Bastian's left arm, or the Webley Brand-Pryce 14.6 millimeter pistol in a blanket roll behind the horse's saddle.

'Are you a town official of some kind?' Bastian's deep, low voice came to the inquisitive local.

'Why, no. It's just that we got this crazy killer in town. Some misfit kid from the Staked Plains. He shot a man's ear off last night, for fun. Then he raped one of our women.'

11

'Why don't you do something about it?'

Before the man could respond Bastian turned, climbed three steps to the saloon, and pushed through the swing door.

There were several patrons inside, at tables and at the long bar. There was a dusty, cracked mirror hanging behind the bar, and on the back wall there was a scarred piano and a poster announcing house rules. An obese bartender was drying shot glasses with a soiled cloth.

Everybody stopped talking when Bastian entered and sat down at a nearby table. A man at a rear table leaned forward to a companion.

'Good Jesus. Somebody's in trouble. That's the Preacher.'

The bartender had walked over to Bastian. 'What's your poison tonight, stranger?' Not knowing his identity.

Bastian gave him a cool look. 'You have any unwatered planter's rye back there?'

A sour response. 'We got the best whiskey in Greer County, mister.'

'Bring the bottle. Listen. Do you expect the Cheyenne Kid in here tonight?'

12

The barkeep frowned as the other customers exchanged dark looks. The man at the rear who had recognized Bastian earlier took a last quick swig of the drink before him.

'I'm getting to hell out of here!' he said in a harsh whisper.

The fellow rose quickly, threw some coins on to the table, and hurried past Bastian and the bartender to the door, followed closely by his companion.

The bartender glanced at them as they hurried past, then turned back to Bastian.

'Yeah, he'll be in. Raising hell. Driving my customers out. What's it to you, stranger?'

'What time does he usually get here?' Bastian said.

'Say, I ain't no information bureau, mister.'

Bastian raised his icy-cold gaze to the barman, but said nothing. When the barkeep saw the look, his breath began coming short.

'He got here the last couple nights at about seven.'

Bastian drew a pocket watch from his trousers and saw it said 6:36. He replaced it and nodded.

'Good. I have time for a meal. You serve food, don't you?'

'Not really. Why don't you go down to the stage depot? They serve just about anything you'd want.'

The two men at the bar had been talking among themselves. Now they, too, hurried out the door. The only customers now were two men on a side wall who were more curious than cautious.

'What do you have here?' Bastian was asking.

'I could fry you up some eggs.'

'Fine. Change the rye to beer and make it a half-dozen eggs over easy.' The bartender nodded, but just stood there. 'Hey. You ain't going up against the Kid, are you?'

Bastian regarded him darkly again. 'Just fill my order.'

'He's killed a dozen men. Some of them sheriffs. Nobody's ever beat him. He's a half-breed, you know. Part Cheyenne, they say. If you're one of them bounty boys, the only thing you'll get is six feet of ground at Boot Hill.'

Bastian slid the Colt from the holster at his belly, and spun the cylinder. Not looking at the barkeep: 'The eggs in ten minutes. Or I blow a hole in your liver.'

The barman swallowed hard, and his face changed. 'Sure. Yes, sir.'

At seven o'clock Bastian was still eating when the Cheyenne Kid came in. He was a stout young man, broad-coupled and muscular, looking very physical. He wore a Colt Navy revolver low on his right hip, and he was reputed to be very good with it. It looked menacing as he stopped just inside the doors and stared a moment at Bastian, narrowing black eyes on him.

He swaggered over to the bar and leaned on it. 'I'm been thirsty ever since I visited that Morris widow last night.' A hard, rather psychotic grin. 'Bring me a red-top rye, and make it a double. Who the hell is that over there?'

The unexpected question at the end

disoriented the bartender. 'Huh?'

The Kid threw a thumb toward Bastian, without turning. 'Him, moron. The undertaker.'

'Oh. Him. Well, he's no undertaker, Kid.'

The Kid's curiosity turned him around, and he assessed Bastian openly and arrogantly.

'Well? If you ain't an undertaker, maybe you're a Bible thumper! Speak up, dandy!'

Only two customers remained now, at a side-wall table, and their curiosity had gotten the better of their caution. They drank tensely and watched. Bastian had finished the eggs, and now took a last swig of his beer.

'I'm Luther Bastian. And you, I guess, are the Cheyenne Kid.'

'That's right, fancy boy. I've killed fifteen men, raped their women and stole their money. I'm wanted by sheriffs in five counties and two banks and a railroad put rewards out on me. What do you think of that?'

Bastian sat back on his chair. 'I think you're a murdering thief and rapist, and you've outlived your time in this world.'

For several seconds there was no sound at all in the room, as the Kid's face fell into hard lines.

'Well, maybe you think you can do something about that, fancy boy.'

'Maybe,' Bastian said easily.

The Kid's face burst into a glittery brightness and a loud laugh issued from his throat. He turned to the bar.

'Did you hear that, barkeep? Fancy boy over there don't seem to like me.'

'Kid,' the bartender said quietly, 'that there is the Preacher. Maybe you'd like to take it outside.' Nervously.

That still meant nothing to the Kid. But the two men at the side wall exchanged a look, rose from their chairs, and moved in opposite directions away from their table, to get out of the line of fire. At the same time, the Kid drew the Colt on his hip while facing the bar, turned and leveled it on Bastian.

'What does that mean? Preacher?'

Bastian didn't flinch. 'That's what some call me. I go after men with bounties on their heads, Kid.'

The Kid's eyes went crazy-looking. 'By God!! You're one of them yellow-belly weasels, you pond scum!'

Bastian only smiled. 'I've never shot a man I didn't give a fair chance to kill me.'

The Kid looked fierce now. 'I see that pea-shooter on your belly there. Take it out and lay it on the table. Slow like.'

Bastian hesitated, then drew the Peacemaker from its oiled holster, and laid it carefully on the table. So casually that he could have been dealing a hand of poker. 'Is that what you wanted?'

The Kid walked over to the table. 'Yeah, cow-dung. That's what I wanted.' He picked the revolver up and examined it, then laughed in his throat. 'You cut this back! You ruined a good gun. What the hell for?'

'So it would fit this special holster,' Bastian replied with a half-smile. 'Any other silly questions?'

A deep frown etched itself on to the Kid's hard face. He took the Colt over to the bar, laid it down there, and turned back to Bastian. The bartender and the two customers watched breathlesly.

'Now, yellow belly. I'm going to make it nice and slow for you. I'll bust your kneecaps first. Maybe put one in that yellow belly. Then I'm going to explode your black heart like a desert melon.'

Bastian grunted. 'I'm sorry to hear that. Especially since I came after you on false information.'

The Kid's finger tightened on the trigger of his Navy Colt. 'I don't care why you came here, lily-liver.'

'I thought you'd want to know. They dropped the reward on you, Kid. Turns out you're not worth anything to authorities now. You're small fry.'

'That's a damn lie!' the Kid bellowed. 'My name is mentioned in whispers on the damn railroad! Two banks doubled their guards and stopped shipments of silver, by Jesus!'

'I have the latest dodger here in my pocket,' Bastian continued calmly. 'Here, you can have it.'

It all happened so quickly and with such calm that the Kid didn't try to stop it. His curiosity overcame his very marginal concern over the man in the dark clothing. Bastian slid his hand into his coat, found the Meriden pocket revolver in its hidden holster there, and withdrew it in a smooth motion. In the next split second the small sidearm exploded violently in the quiet of the room and hot lead hit the Kid in the left eye, traveled through his brainpan, and blew the back of his skull off.

With Bastian's gun still smoking the Kid just stood there, motionless for a moment. Then his jaw began working, and a jumble of unintelligible words came pouring from his mouth. His Colt then fired loudly; the shot sang past Bastian's right ear and smashed a whiskey glass on the table the two customers had just vacated. The Kid then fell forward on to his face, hitting the floor so hard it shook with his weight.

'Holy Jesus!' one of the customers breathed softly.

The bartender stared hard at Bastian. 'How did you do that?'

Bastian rose from his chair, walked over to the Kid, prone on the floor, and aimed the Meriden at his head a second time. But when he saw the bloody mess that was the Kid's hatless head, he re-holstered the revolver. He picked up his custom Colt Peacemaker from the bar, twirled it twice in his hand, and let it nestle back into the holster on his belly.

The bartender whistled between his teeth.

The two customers, both local farmers, came forward now, wide-eyed and relieved.

'You just saved this town a lot of grief, mister,' the taller of the two spoke up. Bastian took a piece of paper from his pocket without responding.

'This is an affidavit. Identifying the Kid and saying I killed him. I'd appreciate it if you all signed it before I leave. It's for the authorities.'

They all nodded numbly. A few minutes later they had all signed the paper and it was back in Bastian's pocket. He turned to the bartender, and threw some coins on to the bar.

'How far is it to Fort Griffin?'

The bartender shrugged, still staring down at the corpse of the Kid. The second customer intervened, though.

'It's a short day's ride, Preacher.'

'The name is Bastian,' the dark-suited man corrected him.

The fellow looked embarrased. 'Yes, sir.'

Bastian sighed. 'Maybe I'll start tonight,' he said to himself. He took one last look at the bartender. 'You're one lucky barkeep, mister. That beer was one notch above trough water. But I'm in a good mood tonight.'

Then he left with all three staring after him.

*   *   *

The evening was still young in Medicine Bend, a couple hours' ride to the

22

north of Stinking Creek. Simon Gabriel had been surprised by the substantial look of the town, with its two stores, small hotel, and prosperous-looking saloon. Gabriel wondered if there was money to be had in this remote Texas settlement before he took his gang back into Indian Territory.

The gang had taken the entire floor of the Mary Lou Hotel, named for the owner's wife. They were not welcome, but the owner knew better than to refuse six gun-toting outlaws. So they took over the hotel that afternoon, demanding service and food. The management complied with little hope of being compensated for the trouble.

Jonah Spencer had seen the gang ride in and knew immediately who they were. It was Jonah who ran into Mayor Purvis's house and reported the gang's arrival to him. Purvis muttered some obscenities that Jonah had never heard before, and decided to keep well away from the Prairie Schooner saloon where some of the gang were now drinking, in early evening. So far Gabriel hadn't paid for any drinks that were ordered.

Gabriel sat at a table with Cuckoo Bobo and Cottonwood Eddie; there were a few other patrons present, but most had left when Gabriel showed up. There was a slim, nervous-looking bartender arranging cases of beer being brought in by a stockboy from a back room.

'You know, I like the looks of this little backwater,' Gabriel was telling his subordinates. 'I'd guess a man could find himself some hard cash behind the doors of those whitewashed houses. There's no law here. We could persuade the mayor to levy a tax for us. Like we did last year in Missouri.'

'We owned that town,' Bobo spoke up in a reedy voice. He swigged from a shot glass of whiskey. He was a rather short, meaty-looking fellow with soiled clothing and a crossed left eye. His real name was Henry Bobo, and he had killed his own mother at the age of sixteen in a fit of psychotic rage. He carried a Tranter Army .45 on his right hip, and would draw it for the slightest reason. He had recently killed a man in Stillwater for asking about his left eye.

'This place looks even better,' Cottonwood Eddie offered. 'I'd bet there's a small fortune in them store cash boxes.' He was almost six feet tall, just under Gabriel's height, and had dirty-blond, strawlike hair under a trail-colored hat. His eyes were small and squinty-looking and watery. The law had found him once sleeping under a cottonwood tree, and made an easy arrest, long before he joined up with Gabriel.

His ambition was to open up his own brothel. His real name was Edward Guthrie and he was a stone-cold killer who wanted to be rich, with or without Gabriel.

'But I say we take all we can get and go. We can waste a lot of time in a place like this. We should be going after banks, Simon. That's where the real money is.'

Gabriel shot him a hard look. 'Are you getting ideas about running this show, Eddie?' A long Colt Army .38 hung prominently on his belt.

Eddie looked up warily. 'Hell, no, Simon. You're the boss here. But I got my own opinions about things. Right?'

'Just keep them to yourself,' Gabriel growled at him. He was six feet tall and rather brawny, tough-looking with a scar running down the side of his face. He had a grating, low voice and emanated an aura of authority. He was wearing a bright-red kerchief on his neck, but his clothing was otherwise nondescript. He liked taking over a town and making it his for a while. It gave him a feeling of power for which he had always thirsted.

'Where's Rueda? Did he stay back at the hotel with Thelma and Daddy?'

'He said he had a sick stomach,' Bobo said. 'I think he ate too much of them Mexican *frijoles refritos* at Stinking Creek.'

'Go get him,' Gabriel said. 'I want you and him to go find the mayor and bring him here. I got things to propose to him.'

'Tonight? I got drinking to do,

Simon. And it's all free.' A wild grin.

'There'll be plenty of time for that,' Gabriel said sharply to him. 'Now do what I told you. Now.'

Bobo was gone a couple of minutes later, and he followed Gabriel's orders. He went to Purvis's house with Pedro Rueda. Big Thelma and Sweet Daddy were sharing one of the hotel rooms at the time, and had left a Do Not Disturb sign on the door. Since Sweet Daddy was known to like men instead of women, nobody ever knew what they might be doing when they arranged those private moments, and nobody had asked.

Pedro Rueda was a hard-bitten Mexican who despised Daddy and barely tolerated Thelma's presence in the gang. He was a swarthy man who wore a dark suit with silver buttons. He had a black mustache that he groomed carefully and regularly. He and Bobo found Ethan Purvis in his stable, where he had just brought Jonah some fresh bedding for the cot there. He and Jonah both looked up in surprise when the two men walked in. The mayor's face then registered dismay.

'Oh, there you are,' Bobo said loudly. 'You're the mayor, I reckon.'

Purvis looked them over, and Jonah came over beside him.

'Yes, I'm the mayor. And you're Gabriel's men.'

'That is right, Señor Mayor.' Rueda scowled at him. 'Our boss wants to see you. He's at the Prairie Schooner. You make some time for him, yes?'

'He wants to talk,' Bobo chimed in. 'You know. Have a nice little sit-down with you.'

'I can't imagine why,' Purvis replied. 'I have no business with him.'

'He thinks you do,' Rueda said pointedly. 'You better come, Mr Mayor. For your own good.'

'For your own good,' Bobo said.

'The mayor don't have to go to the saloon with you!' Jonah blurted out. 'He's the mayor here. Tell Gabriel he can come here.'

'Shut up, little *muchacho*,' Rueda growled at him. 'And keep out of the way.'

Jonah noticed the Remington .44 hanging big and ominous on Rueda's gunbelt, and decided not to speak further.

'It's all right, boy,' Purvis assured him. 'I won't be gone long. You run in and tell the missus where I am.'

Jonah nodded doubtfully. He hadn't liked living in Purvis's stable much, and was beginning to wish there were a way to get to his aunt in the Territory. But he liked Purvis.

'I'll tell her, Mr Mayor.'

A few minutes later the three arrived at the saloon. Gabriel, still sitting with Eddie, saw Purvis immediately. He rose from his chair.

'Ah, it's the mayor! Glad you could join us, Purvis. Come on over and sit with us. We're buying.'

Purvis reluctantly went over and sat with the two outlaws, not knowing what to expect. Rueda and Cuckoo Bobo sat at a nearby table, and ordered drinks for both tables.

Gabriel was all smiles. When the drinks came he held a shot glass high.

'To the prosperity of Medicine Bend,' he said loudly.

'To Medicine Bend,' echoed Cotton-wood Eddie.

There were no customers in the place now except for the outlaws and Purvis. Everybody had left, uncomfortable with the presence of the gang. Purvis didn't want the whiskey offered him, but figured it was smart to accept the toast.

'To our fair town,' he said reluctantly, and quaffed the drink.

'Now,' Gabriel said to him, 'let's get down to business, Purvis. You've got a nice little town here, and a nice little job running it. We just thought we might give you some help with managing the whole thing. It must be a big job for one man.'

'I get the job done,' Purvis said quietly. 'What's this all about, Gabriel?'

Gabriel looked down at the table soberly. 'I'm going to be honest with you, Purvis. My boys wanted to wreck your little town. Steal from the cash boxes. Look your women over. Shoot the place up.'

Purvis and he stared at each other

silently for a moment.

'But I told them there's no need for any of that, Mr Mayor. Not if you cooperate with us in the next week or so that we'll be here.'

Purvis sighed heavily. 'What kind of cooperation are you talking about?'

Gabriel's eyebrows shot up to form an innocent look. 'Nothing violent. Nothing even illegal. In your official capacity we'd like you to levy a duty on the citizens of Medicine Bend. An emergency measure. Like if a storm was coming. An ounce of prevention . . . you know the adage. I'd guess most residents will be happy to pay a little something to avert a disaster.'

Another heavy silence. After a moment, the bartender behind the counter muttered, 'Oh, oh.' Then he gestured for the stockboy to return to the back room and leave.

'I've heard about your habit of forcing your 'tax' levies,' Purvis said with a somber face. 'That won't work here in Texas, Gabriel.'

'Of course it will. We'll only ask, let's say . . . twenty-five dollars from each citizen. Almost everybody has that much to spare. You'll nail up posters and circulate flyers. The plan will have your backing, and people will listen to you. My boys will do the collecting. Then we'll patronize your saloons and stores before going on our way. In a couple weeks we'll just be a bad memory.' A friendly grin that didn't quite come off.

'What you'll do is bleed this town dry and then ride out with your saddle-bags full of our money,' Purvis told him. 'I can't be a part of that, Gabriel.' He thought of his wife, waiting for him. He thought of the good life he had here in this town he loved. Then he went on. 'Shoot me if you have to. But I won't betray my town.'

Gabriel sighed heavily, and sat back on his chair. 'Well. What do you think of that, boys? We got ourselves a damn hero here.'

Cuckoo Bobo rose menacingly from the next table. 'I say we don't need him.' He drew the Tranter at his hip and leveled it at Purvis's head. 'He can only be trouble for us now. Let me have him.'

'Take him out back to do it,' Rueda suggested, swigging some liquor.

Cottonwood Eddie shook his head. 'If there was a bank here, we'd be getting drunk in the Territory by now.'

'Put the gun away, Bobo,' Gabriel said.

Bobo gave him a sour look, then obeyed. He muttered something inaudible, went over to the bar and ordered another drink. The slim bartender served him without breathing.

'I'm not going to shoot you, Mayor,' Gabriel finally told him. 'I'm going to persuade you to accept our proposal. That's civilized, isn't it?'

Purvis eyed him narrowly. 'I'm no danger to you. And I won't change my mind. Just let me go back home.'

'Well, I think I ought to at least have a chance to change your mind.' Gabriel smiled. He looked around the room, and saw an interior post that supported hand-hewn rafters up above. 'Bobo, take the good mayor over there and tie him to that post.'

Bobo frowned with curiosity. 'Hell. Whatever you say, Simon.'

'For God's sake,' Eddie muttered, but so that Gabriel couldn't hear him.

Purvis had no choice but to comply. In just moments he was tied to the post, and Gabriel was facing him on his chair.

'There. Now we're going to have a little shooting match, Mayor. You can stop it any time you want to. Eddie, go get a shot glass and place it on the mayor's head.'

'I'm the mayor of a Texas town, Gabriel. You'll answer to the law for this.'

Gabriel laughed. 'Law? What law? Go ahead, Eddie.'

'This doesn't entertain me,' Eddie replied. 'I'm heading back to the hotel, Simon. See if I can find Thelma.' He rose from his chair.

Gabriel slowly drew the big Colt at his side and aimed it at Eddie. 'Would you rather be tied to that post?'

Eddie frowned heavily at Gabriel.

'What the hell . . . ?'

'Put a glass on his head,' Gabriel said deliberately. 'And take the first shot at it.'

Eddie sighed. He would leave Gabriel one day. Or maybe shoot him. But this wasn't the time. 'All right, all right.'

He procured a shot glass, went and knocked Purvis's hat to the floor, and carefully set the glass on top of Purvis's head. Then he returned to his table, and drew the Iver Johnson from its nest and aimed it at Purvis. Purvis stood at the post, hands tied behind it, and began sweating on his upper lip.

Eddie fired, and the shot shook the rafters. The lead missed the glass narrowly but cut a path through Purvis's hair and thudded into the wall behind him. Gabriel laughed loudly.

'Is that the best you can do, boy? I could do that good with my left hand.' He turned to Bobo. 'OK. You're next. Try not to hit the mayor.' A low chuckle.

At that same moment at the Mary Lou Hotel, a guest was leaving who nobody knew was in town. He had arrived the night before, and had kept to himself, wanting to maintain his privacy. He knew nothing yet of the gang who resided on the floor above his. He intended to stay one more night, after paying his respects to Mayor Purvis this evening. His name was Eli St Clair and he was the Texas Ranger Purvis had mentioned the day he got his wire about Gabriel.

'I plain forgot where Mayor Purvis lives,' he was saying to the hotel clerk as he left. 'Can you point me in the right direction, young man?'

'If you want the mayor, he's down at the Prairie Schooner,' the fellow replied. 'I saw him walk down there with a couple of other men a while ago.'

St Clair nodded and left the hotel. He was a man headed toward middle age, with lines in his face from hard riding in the Texas sun. He wore a Colt Peacemaker much like that of Luther Bastian, but it still had its long barrel.

He heard the second shot taken at Purvis's whiskey glass, and the laughter that followed it, and his brow creased as he climbed some steps and entered the saloon.

Bobo was just holstering his gun. He had missed the glass too, and slightly creased Purvis's scalp. Everybody turned to look at St Clair as he entered. His star-shaped badge showed plainly on his vest.

'Oh, for God's sake,' Gabriel groaned.

Nobody had a gun out, and St Clair didn't draw his. He had seen Purvis tied to the post as soon as he was in the room.

'Well, boys. Having yourselves a little fun here?'

Bobo was still standing. His gaze darted to Gabriel for instructions. But Gabriel shook his head.

'Oh, we're just entertaining the mayor some, mister. Say, are you with the Rangers?'

'Have been for quite a while,' St Clair replied coolly. 'Maybe it's time for the fun to be over. What do you say, Mr Mayor?'

Purvis nodded weakly. Blood had inched from his hair down the side of his face. 'Thanks.'

'I hope you won't mind,' St Clair said to Gabriel. He recognized him from a Wanted poster. 'The mayor is an old friend of mine.'

He walked over casually and cut Purvis loose with a small pocket knife. He examined the cut in Purvis's scalp.

'You got a nasty scratch there, Mayor. Why don't you go on home and get that looked after?'

Purvis nodded numbly. 'I will. I'll . . . see you later.'

'At your house,' St Clair agreed.

Neither Gabriel nor his men disputed the exit, and in a short moment, Purvis was gone. Gabriel had given up on forcing him, anyway. Now St Clair turned to Gabriel and drew his Colt. Bobo went for his gun, too, and again Gabriel stopped him.

'You're Simon Gabriel,' St Clair said levelly. 'I saw the dodger on you. I don't know about these others, I'll check them out before I leave town. But I got to place you under arrest.'

Gabriel grunted. 'I heard you boys got a lot of brass. But don't you think you're biting off a little more than you can digest, Mr Ranger?'

St Clair noticed that Bobo, who was back at the bar, was beyond St Clair's peripheral vision. 'Would you step around here, mister, where I can see you?' the Ranger asked him pleasantly.

Bobo grunted out a low laugh in his throat, and moved forward into St Clair's view.

'Thank you,' St Clair said. 'Now, Gabriel. I'm kind of used to biting off big mouthfuls that are hard to get down. I arrested John Ringo once, over in Abilene. Before I pinned this badge on I rode shotgun on one of the most dangerous stage trails in the Missouri Breaks. I'm not afraid of your guns. Now, why don't you just walk over to the hotel with me, and I'll find a nice comfortable place for you to sleep tonight until I can send a wire off tomorrow morning.'

Gabriel saw that the long Colt was still aimed at his chest, and hesitated before he spoke again.

'Look, boy. I don't care if you brought in Jesse James. If you try to use that Colt on me, three men here will start filling you with lead.'

St Clair walked over to him and put the muzzle of the Colt up against Gabriel's right temple. 'Well, that won't do you any good, will it?'

Gabriel's face showed fear for the first time. But St Clair had violated a cardinal rule in repositioning himself. His back was now to the door. And in the next moment, Big Thelma stepped in quietly behind him. She was a large woman, with features that were more masculine than feminine. She was the best shot in the gang.

St Clair didn't know she was there yet. She glanced at Gabriel, drew a Harrington & Richardson .38 revolver from her waistband and fired it just as St Clair sensed her presence and began turning around. The hot slug caught

40

him behind the left ear and blew part of his face away. He gasped audibly and then was stumbling across the room, firing the Colt and knocking a chair over as he tumbled headlong to the floor.

The acrid smell of gunsmoke filled the room as Thelma casually slid the revolver back into the black-and-gold holster at her waist. She walked to the bar. 'Make it a double rye, barkeep,' she said in a deep voice. Then she turned to Gabriel and smiled.

'And the boys wonder why I keep you on.' Gabriel grinned.

There was a low moan from St Clair, even though he was almost dead. That caught Bobo's attention; he walked over to the near lifeless figure, studied it for a moment, then ripped the star off St Clair's vest.

'This will look great in my trophy box,' Bobo grinned, holding the badge up for all to see.

But as he looked at the silver star, Gabriel's face sobered. 'Put the damned thing away,' he said in a hard voice.

Bobo frowned. He hesitated, shrugged, and slipped the badge into a vest pocket. But there was a wild, resentful look just behind his eyes.

'Now,' Gabriel went on, 'haul that body into the back room where I can't see it. I'll have to give this some more thought.'

The corpse of the Texas Ranger was dragged from the bar room by Bobo and Rueda, leaving a narrow but clear trail of crimson on the wood floor.

2

'St Clair was one of our best,' the young man with the star on his chest murmured gravely. 'I was hoping to do some drinking with him when he arrived back here.'

He was sitting slumped on a chair facing Captain Brett Mallory, with Mallory's desk between them. His name was Riley, and he and the captain were Texas Rangers.

Mallory nodded. 'The wire came from the mayor at Medicine Bend. He says Gabriel's gang is bragging about it. By God, nobody murders a Texas Ranger and brags about it!' He was clasping and unclasping his hands before him, leaning on the desk. Behind him in one corner was an American flag, and in the other the Lone Star flag of Texas.

'We have to do something about it, Captain.'

Mallory let a long breath out. 'I'm stretched to breaking point right now. Austin won't approve any hiring.'

'Send me,' Riley said. 'I'll deal with them.' Innocence in his face.

Mallory looked over at him. 'You against six gunmen? I don't send anybody on suicide missions, Riley. Anyway, with this recent influx of crooked gamblers I need you right here in Dallas. It would take a small posse to go after Gabriel with any chance of success against him.' He rubbed at his chin. 'Eli and I go back fifteen years, Riley. He never wanted a promotion. He liked being out there, he said, where the action is. Then he walks into that hornet's nest. He wasn't even on assignment. He was heading back here.'

He sat there thinking. He was a blocky, square-faced fellow with mostly gray hair and a broken nose from an early saloon fight. His gunbelt hung on a hat rack near the door.

'I just don't know what I can do. Maybe we could free up a few men in Abilene in a couple weeks. But Gabriel might be gone by then. I hear he likes the Indian Territory.'

'Maybe you could get authority to hire some men. Just for this job. Hey, that reminds me. I saw that bounty hunter at Watson's store yesterday. That one that dresses like he was headed for a funeral.'

Mallory grunted out a small laugh. 'That's Luther Bastian. I know him well. When I was town marshal ten years ago, in Fort Griffin, Bastian was my deputy. That boy knows more about guns than any man I've ever met. But he's got a dark side. Very private, almost anti-social. Before he came to me his younger brother was murdered by thieves while alone in their cabin. They messed him up pretty bad. Bastian went after them, on his own, and killed all three of them. I think that's why he became a lawman.'

'But then he quit that.'

'I think he figured he was hamstrung by rules, wearing a badge. He has a deep hatred for men like Simon Gabriel. And of course, he makes good money with the bounties, too. Word has it that he won't go after a man who doesn't have at least five thousand on his head. And God help the man he goes after, because he's never arrested one. So maybe it's appropriate that he wears funerary garb.'

Riley smiled. 'Sounds like a man I'd like to meet.'

Mallory shook his head. 'I doubt it. He probably wouldn't give you the time of day. The man doesn't seem to like anybody. But if I wanted somebody dead, I'd call on Bastian in a minute.'

'Then why not call on him now?' Riley wondered.

Mallory laughed. 'Bastian would never pin a badge on again. Not even a lone star. Maybe especially not a lone star.'

'I didn't mean that. Persuade him to go after Gabriel for the bounties.'

Mallory started to laugh again, but then stared at his hands in silence. 'The Bureau has never worked with a bounty hunter. And the bounties aren't substantial enough on Gabriel's gang.'

'Maybe you could do something about that.'

Mallory was thinking again. 'Hmm. I wonder if he's still in town. It couldn't hurt to talk to him. Why don't you check out the hotels in the vicinity of that store, Riley, and tell Bastian I'd like to see him here in my office. For old times' sake.'

Riley smiled and rose. 'I'll get right on it.'

★　★　★

Luther Bastian was oiling his Winchester rifle when Ranger Riley knocked on his hotel-room door. He met him at the door impatiently.

'What the hell is it?' He looked different from that night in Sloan's Crossroads. He was in his shirtsleeves and the shirt was open at the neck. But he carried the custom Colt in his right hand. You never knew who might knock on your door.

'I'm John Riley, of the Texas Rangers,' Riley announced brightly. 'Captain Mallory wants to know if you'll see him at his office.'

Bastian hesitated, then replied, 'No.' He closed the door in Riley's face.

He had got halfway back to the bed where he had been sitting when Riley knocked again.

'Go away,' Bastian called out.

'Please, Mr Bastian. It's kind of urgent.'

Bastian sighed, and returned to the door, without the Colt. He opened it to Riley's smiling face.

'He really needs you. He said, for old times,' said the Ranger.

Bastian looked the young fellow up and down. 'Are you even out of school?'

Riley's face flushed some. 'Of course. I've been a Ranger for over a year.'

'Is Mallory there now?'

Riley nodded. 'I just left him.'

'Tell him I'll be right over. And you ought to wear that Colt three inches lower on your hip. It will make an easier draw.'

Riley looked down at his sidearm. 'OK. Thanks, Mr Bastian. I'll tell him you're coming.'

It was only a half-hour later when Luther Bastian entered Brett Mallory's large office. Mallory met him at the door.

'I'll be damned! The many reports of your demise must have been premature, Luther.' A hearty handshake. 'Come on in and sit.'

'You're looking well, Brett. And you've come up in the world.'

They seated themselves as Mallory looked Bastian over.

'By Jesus! You do look formidable in that outfit. You making any money?' he asked.

'I keep my head above water,' Bastian told him. 'I do a lot better than we did, back in Fort Griffin.'

'I think back on all that sometimes and wish I was back there,' Mallory said. 'Things seemed simpler then.'

'We put some people where they belong,' Bastian offered. He studied Mallory's broad face. 'What is it, Brett? Why did you send for me?'

Mallory sighed. 'A bunch of lowlifes

killed one of my men up in Medicine Bend. Eli St Clair, an old friend of mine. I got to do something about it, Luther.'

'You're out of manpower up that way?'

Mallory nodded. 'We never had much. I can't respond to this directly, I just don't have the people. I wondered if I could interest you.'

Bastian frowned. 'Who killed him?'

'Simon Gabriel and his gang. I hear there are six in all now.'

Bastian nodded. 'There are. He's gathered a real bunch of crazies around him. But they don't interest me, if that's what you're getting at. Gabriel is worth two thousand, and the rest are thousand-dollar wants. I wouldn't waste my time. I'm not a lawman any more, Brett.'

'I wouldn't ask you to pin a badge on again,' Mallory said. 'But what if the stakes were higher?'

Bastian narrowed his dark eyes on Mallory. 'How much higher?'

'Gabriel recently held up a small bank in Fort Worth. Didn't get much, but he made that rich little bank nervous. Threatened to come back. We think he'll return to the Territory next, but the bank doesn't know that. I could hint he's thinking of returning to their area.'

Bastian gave him a rare, sardonic smile. 'Shame on you, Captain.'

'It would be for the bigger good.' A return of the smile. 'I think I can talk their president into placing, say, five thousand apiece on them.'

'Five thousand is my minimum, Brett.'

'But that would be times six,' Mallory reminded him. 'That wouldn't be a bad nest egg.'

'I have a nest egg,' Bastian argued. 'Anyway, I'm pushing forty, Brett. I've been thinking of hanging up the iron. I've got my eye on a nice little piece of land down by the border. Rolling hills. Grassland. A man could raise cattle on it. Frankly, I'm getting a bit tired of all this.'

'The Preacher? Hanging up his hand-customed Colt?'

'You're an old friend. But I'll shoot

51

the next man that calls me that.'

Mallory grinned. 'Sorry. But it would be a red-calendar day for the bad guys.'

Bastian shook his head. 'God, I was just up there, Brett. I've been planning on spending some time in the city now.'

'I know it's a hell of a lot to ask. You against a pack of wolves like them. I could send Riley with you. He likes you.'

Bastian gave him a look. 'And have to worry about him, too? No, thanks.'

Mallory sighed. 'I need you bad, Luther. Texas needs you. What they did can't go unanswered. If you don't go, I might have to.'

Bastian frowned at him. 'You been behind a desk too long, *compadre*.' He looked out a nearby window, soberly. 'The posters would have to say Dead or Alive.'

Mallory's face brightened. 'I know. That's the way I would want it.'

'I understand one of them is a woman. I've never killed a woman.'

'She's the one that murdered St Clair,' Mallory said.

Bastian's face revealed his surprise. 'Well.'

'So you'll do it?' Mallory said expectantly.

Bastian blew a breath out. 'Maybe I'll make it my last big piece of business before I buy that ranchland. You're sure the bank is good for the money?'

'I'm positive,' Mallory said firmly. 'I'll have it all arranged before you arrive up there.'

Bastian nodded. 'I'll leave tomorrow.'

Mallory rose and extended his hand warmly. 'Congratulations, partner! You just became the left hand of the by-God Texas Rangers.'

Bastian took his hand reluctantly. 'How nice for me,' he replied acidly.

*   *   *

Jonah Spencer was on his way in from the stable to see Ethan Purvis that same afternoon, reflecting on recent events as he walked. He had grown up a lot in the past couple of days. He had seen the mayor of Medicine Bend humiliated, and a halo-wearing Texas Ranger shot to death by dangerous men. He hadn't believed any of that possible, and he was still in shock over those world-shaking calamities.

When he arrived inside the house, Purvis was sitting at a kitchen table with his head in his hands. His wife was upstairs in bed, where she had spent most of her time since the shooting, debilitated physically and emotionally.

'It's me, Mr Mayor,' Jonah said, announcing his presence.

Purvis looked up at him. He hadn't paid Jonah much attention since that night at the saloon.

'Oh. What do you want, boy?' His face was sallow, his expression impassive.

'I was just wondering if the missus was going to fix supper tonight. I haven't had much to eat today.'

Purvis looked bewildered. The gouge on his scalp where he had been shot in the gang's target practice was healing now, and was scabbing over.

'Supper? Oh, I don't know, Jonah. She ain't herself today. Here.' He reached into a pocket and laid two seated liberty quarters on the table. 'Get yourself something over at the store.'

Jonah looked at the quarters and picked them up with a sigh. 'Can I get you anything, sir? Make you a cup of coffee?'

'No, Jonah. It's my stomach. You go on to the store and buy yourself something good. I'll be all right.'

'Mr Mayor. I don't like it here any more. I'm going to leave.'

Already, the Gabriel gang had killed another man. The hotel clerk had asked for a payment up front for rental of the entire top floor, and Sweet Daddy, under the influence of a peyote cigarette, had shot the clerk through his prairie-flowered vest. Daddy, whose real name was Dadieau Rochambert, was, despite his oftimes effeminate tendencies, the fastest draw in the gang, which was the reason Gabriel kept him on. Cottonwood Eddie had relieved the cash boxes at both general stores of their contents, and Cuckoo Bobo had raped a sixteen-year-old girl who lived with an aging uncle. And Luther Gabriel himself was still making plans to exact some kind of tribute from the town.

Purvis seemed to really see Jonah for the first time. 'What? Leave? What are you talking about, boy?'

Jonah looked down. 'This is a different town now. I mean, even if they go, I don't want to be here any more. I got nobody here. I'm going to Kiowa Junction. To my aunt. I've always wanted to see the Territory.'

Purvis dragged himself up out of the doldrums. 'Now you listen to me, Jonah. There'a no way to get you to your aunt right now. I'll have to figure all that out. When my head gets clear again.'

Jonah stuck his chin out. 'I'm going. I'll take one of your horses in the middle of the night if you won't help me. I hate this place now. It's spoiled for me. A Texas Ranger was killed here, Mr Mayor. And nobody's doing anything about it.'

'If you left like that, Jonah, I'd have to come after you. And I would. I'd bring you back here till you can travel safely to your aunt. Do you want to put me through that? With the trouble I already have?'

Jonah's eyes teared up. 'I guess not. You been good to me.'

Purvis reached out and touched his hand. 'Listen. I'll get you to your aunt. I promise you that. Just give me some time, Jonah. Will you?'

Before Jonah could reply a knocking came at the open door, and then Pedro Rueda walked in, uninvited.

'*Buenas tardes*, Señor Mayor! How is that scratch in your scalp healing?'

Purvis's heart sank. He had hoped to be left alone until Gabriel decided he had had his fill of Medicine Bend.

'I'm doing fine, Rueda. What do you want?'

Rueda ignored the question, and glanced over at Jonah, standing beside the kitchen table.

'Hey. Who is this *muchacho*?'

'I'm Jonah Spencer, you murderer,' Jonah said angrily.

Rueda's face developed a scowl.

'Take it easy, boy,' Purvis said quietly.

'What do you know of me, little coyote?' Rueda said acidly. He was a sociopath with no feelings for others except disdain. He was deadly with his Remington .44.

'Why don't you all just go and leave us alone?' Jonah blurted out.

Now Rueda decided to laugh softly. He turned to Purvis. 'Gabriel wants a little favor of you, Mr Mayor.'

'I told him. I won't be a part of his plans.'

'This isn't about that. You have a few women of the evening here in this rat-trap of a town, *sí*? You know, *putas*.'

'I wouldn't know,' Purvis told him.

'Well, I am sure you do. You round them up and bring them to the Schooner. Just to drink with us while we are here, you know. And Gabriel says he wants you to make him a loan.'

'What?'

'You must have some cash around here. And there must be town money. Gabriel says if you can lend him five thousand dollars, that might encourage him to leave your little town sooner.'

'I don't have that kind of money.'

'You have friends, Mr Mayor. Many friends, I am *cierto*. You can get it together, if you really want to.' His voice changed. 'It's very important to you, *señor*.'

Purvis looked up at him and asessed the warning in his face. Then he answered soberly, 'Important to me?'

'You take my meaning, *yo creo*. You might call it a matter of life or death.' A hard grin.

Jonah was suddenly red-faced with anger. 'Leave him alone, you yellow greaser! Get out of his house,' he shouted, then stood there, breathing heavily.

'Jonah!' Purvis warned him.

But the warning came too late. With an easy swing of his arm, Rueda back-handed Jonah across the face, the slap sounding loud in the room and sending Jonah flying against the nearby wall. He smacked hard there, but didn't fall. He stood there stunned, his cheek blazing, his eyes tearing. But he wouldn't cry. Not in front of this hated man.

Purvis rose from the table quickly, wanting to throw himself at Rueda. But he knew that could be suicide.

'Damn you! You're also a child-beater?'

'He didn't hurt me,' Jonah lied to protect Purvis. He put his hand to his cheek.

'Maybe you must teach this coyote cub some manners, heh?' Rueda commented smoothly. He leaned toward Purvis. 'Gabriel will expect the loan by noon tomorrow, Mr Mayor. Noon tomorrow.'

He departed without giving Jonah another look.

Purvis went over to the boy then, and examined his face. 'You'll be all right. I'll get you a cold cloth.'

'I don't want a cold cloth,' Jonah said in a broken voice. He turned from Purvis and ran from the house, back to the stable, while Purvis stared after him.

But Purvis didn't have much time to think about Jonah. He spent the rest of that day counting up his assets, and calling on a few close friends, men who had helped put him in office years ago. By day's end he had raised over $3,500, and he hoped that would be enough to send Gabriel on his way. He would present it to the outlaw the following morning.

That evening, however, Jonah Spencer had made his own plans about the gang. When Purvis's wife called him to supper he yelled back that he wasn't hungry. Purvis decided to leave him to himself for a bit, to get past what he had experienced with Rueda earlier.

In mid-evening, Purvis went out to talk with yet another potential contributor to the Gabriel fund and, for a while, his wife was upstairs doing some domestic chores. During that hiatus, Jonah sneaked into the house, went to a small gun cabinet where Purvis kept a loaded Colt revolver, took the gun out and left the house with it.

Too many things were happening in Jonah's life, and too fast. He didn't realize it, but he was still in shock from the death of his grandfather, the man who had raised him. That had left Jonah at sea. And now the rest of his world was falling apart, and all because of these evil men who had come to terrorize his town and humble its mayor. Perhaps the worst shock after losing his grandfather was the death of the Texas Ranger who had tried to help them. Suddenly it seemed as if something had to be done, before everybody went flying off into black space from a spinning-out-of-control world.

It was a short walk to the Prairie Schooner. It was dark when he arrived outside, and he stood listening to the talking and laughter from the saloon. He checked the ammunition in the revolver, and the gun hung at ready in his right hand.

When Jonah entered the saloon nobody even noticed him at first. Once again, the gang had driven other, legitimate customers away, and had taken over the saloon. All six gang members were there this time. Rueda had reported back to Gabriel, and Gabriel was convinced that Purvis would make good on this latest demand, then he could leave this town he had already come to dislike and get back to the Territory, where things had always gone well for him.

Gabriel and Cottonwood Eddie were seated at a table quite near the door, Gabriel's favorite place. Beyond them a short distance, at a second table, were Pedro Rueda and Cuckoo Bobo, playing two-hand poker. Standing at the bar were Sweet Daddy, fairly close to the door, and Big Thelma, a little further down, talking in low tones to the bartender, asking about his liquor stock. The fellow nodded, and headed to a back room.

Gabriel was telling Eddie what he had planned for the gang when they rode back into Indian Territory, and it was Eddie who saw Jonah first. He stopped Gabriel with a gesture, and both men turned their gaze on the boy. When Gabriel went quiet, the rest of the gang saw Jonah too, and just stared hard at him.

Jonah spotted Rueda at the second table, and began walking stoically toward it. He walked right past Sweet Daddy, and stopped near Big Thelma. They had all noticed the Colt by now.

'Well, look at this.' Daddy smiled pleasantly. 'What a handsome boy!'

Thelma watched Jonah come up almost to her elbow, curiosity on her thick face.

'What's up, kid? Where'd you find that gun?'

'I come to kill that Mex,' Jonah said in a harsh, flushed-face voice.

Rueda was facing away from him at the table, and now turned with a curious look. On the far side of the table Bobo began laughing.

'Did you hear that? The kid is going to kill Rueda.'

Now everybody else joined in the laughter, except Gabriel and Eddie at the next table. Jonah raised the Colt; it was heavy in his grasp. He cocked the mechanism with difficulty, and leveled the gun at Rueda.

The laughter stopped. Rueda turned completely around on his chair, and scowled at Jonah.

'I slapped him at Purvis's house.' Then: 'Put the gun down, boy. It's a dangerous toy.'

'He's going to shoot you, Rueda,' Daddy squealed. 'I love it!'

'You better give me the gun, kid,' Thelma suggested, grinning.

But then Jonah squinted his eyes almost shut and squeezed the trigger.

The gun jumped in his hand with the explosion and knocked him backward a half-step. The bullet ripped Rueda's shirt at its collar, and then creased Bobo's scalp just above his left ear, because he sat right behind Rueda.

'*Dios mio!*' Rueda swore loudly, rising from the chair.

There were exclamations from Eddie and Sweet Daddy, and Thelma reached forward and snatched the Colt from Jonah's grasp.

'For God's sake,' Eddie muttered.

Gabriel was just shaking his head. He didn't want anything to upset his apple-cart just yet, with Purvis probably ready to cooperate.

Bobo had felt the burning crease on his scalp, and seen the blood on his finger. His face had gone wild-looking, and he now rose from his chair violently, knocking it over.

'That little weasel!' He drew the Tranter at his side and leveled it at Jonah. 'I'm going to cut you into little pieces, kid!'

As his finger tightened over the trigger, Gabriel barked out a command.

'Don't do it, Bobo!'

The crazed Bobo seemed not to hear him. 'Step off, Thelma, or you might catch some lead,' he warned in a breathless voice.

'Damn it! I said hold it,' Gabriel fairly shouted at him.

Bobo seemed to hear the voice from the far end of a long tunnel. He hesitated, then turned blankly toward Gabriel. He swallowed hard.

'This is my play,' he said, in a harsh, dry voice. Gabriel drew the Colt Army from its holster slowly, and leveled it at Bobo.

'You spoil my plans and I'll kill you.'

The room fell deadly silent with that announcement. At Gabriel's table Eddie hoped Gabriel would shoot Bobo. He had never considered him sane enough to ride with them.

'What the hell, Gabriel?' Bobo said gutturally, the emotion subsiding in him.

Rueda, from across the table, reached out and pushed his hand down on the muzzle of Bobo's revolver. Bobo met his eye. Rueda nodded and Bobo reluctantly slid the big gun back into its holster.

'I wish I'd killed both of you,' Jonah blurted out angrily.

Thelma spun Purvis's Colt in her hand for a moment, assessing its weight. *Out of balance*, she said to herself. Then: 'You better clear out of here, kid. While you still can.'

'You heard her,' Gabriel said. He

holstered his gun. 'Stay clear of here, boy. And you might just survive our visit here.'

'You come back here, I'll cut your ears off!' Bobo yelled at Jonah.

Jonah had never been so disappointed. It took a man, he guessed, to take these bad men down. And there was nobody in Medicine Bend who could do it.

'Some day,' he grated out, 'some day you'll all pay. For everything.'

Then he turned and ran from the saloon, out into the darkness of the night.

3

Fort Griffin was rather quiet that evening. The area cowboys hadn't gotten their pay yet, and most were broke from the previous month, so the saloons were almost empty. Luther Bastian had elected to make the town an overnight stay on his way back to the north, and found a room in a clean little hotel on the main street.

Fort Griffin had a colorful history. Not long ago it had been the site of the renowned Fort Griffin Rendezvous, where hunters, traders, Indians and dealers met on open ground at a big campsite to trade, buy and sell their goods. These consisted of everything from furs and hides to horses, saddlery, guns of all kinds, and personal items. It was a big celebration of success, or lack of it, through the year, and there was drinking, singing, dancing, and trade palavers. To make the most of the reunion a man had to speak five or six Indian languages and French. It would usually last several weeks, and involve shootings, theft, and the making of small fortunes.

There was still an area east of town where smaller trade fairs were still held, and Bastian had ridden through it on his way to town. As a very young man he had attended one of the last big rendezvous, and had won a rifle in a shooting contest.

Now the town was peaceful, almost civilized, unless somebody like Simon Gabriel swept through the area like a blue norther, raising hell and causing trouble.

Those thoughts flitted around in Bastian's head like bats in a cave as he entered the small dining room of the hotel on that evening when Jonah Spencer had confronted the Gabriel gang in Medicine Bend.

There was the odor of frying steaks in the room, and a cooking vegetable,

Bastian couldn't make out exactly what. There were two other patrons there, already eating, and a young waiter hovering at a door to the kitchen. Bastian took a seat at a table nearest the outside door, and the waiter rushed over to him. Both of the other diners, tough-looking men, stopped eating for a moment to appraise Bastian's looks.

'Evening, stranger,' the apron-wearing waiter greeted Bastian. 'Staying at the hotel?'

Bastian looked up at him. 'Would it make any difference in the kind of food you bring me?'

'Why, no, sir.'

'Then what's the importance?' Bastian grunted out. He was tired from his day's ride. 'You got fresh steaks back there somewhere?'

The fellow was very thin, with pimples on his lower face.

'Yes, sir! Them cows was eating hay and bellowing their heads off an hour ago.' He laughed at his own joke, and seemed surprised that it got no reaction from either Bastian or the other customers.

'Bring me one rare, with potatoes and that vegetable I smell cooking back there. And start me off with a pint of your dark ale.'

'All we got is golden-brewed beer.'

Bastian frowned slightly. 'OK, bring what you got.'

Bastian's coat was open, and the custom Colt showed plainly on the front of his gunbelt. The waiter stared at it for a moment, then left for the kitchen. One of the other diners, the older of the two, was finished eating. He looked over at Bastian.

'You just arrive in town today, stranger?'

Bastian turned a slow look on him. 'Yes. Today.'

'Well, it's none of my business. But there's a big poker game starting down at the Lost Dogie tonight. All comers welcome. You look like a man who would enjoy a little sporting pastime.' A big grin. 'I'm part owner in the saloon. Ben

Slocum. I didn't catch your monicker.'

'I never gamble,' Bastian said flatly.

The fellow frowned and looked Bastian over. 'Say, wait. That outfit of yours. You wouldn't be the Preacher, would you?'

Bastian sighed, and cast a heavy scowl on him. 'I said I'd kill the next man who called me that. But if I did, I'd be ahead of Billy the Kid.'

The man's face blanched slightly. 'I apologize, Mr Bastian. That's it, ain't it? Bastian?'

'Are you finished eating, mister?'

The fellow hesitated. 'Why, yes.'

'Than haul your carcass out of here and give me a chance.'

The other man swallowed hard. He rose quickly. 'Sure, Mr Bastian. Anything you say.' He hurried to the door. 'Good to meet you, though.'

He had been gone just a moment when the other patron, a young, brash-looking fellow, turned to Bastian.

'So you're the famous Preacher.'

Bastian turned a hostile look on him.

'I have to tell you. You don't look like somebody to be scared of, mister.'

'Fine,' Bastian responded quietly. The waiter came out and delivered Bastian's beer, and Bastian swigged some down. 'Now let me drink my beer in silence.'

But the young man, a wild cow-puncher from a local ranch, now rose arrogantly and faced Bastian squarely.

'I don't think it's right you drive a man out of here just because he calls your name. Like you just done to that Slocum.'

The waiter was still in the room, over by the kitchen. He looked scared.

'Don't cause no trouble in here, Ned. He's just passing through.'

'How's that steak coming?' Bastian asked curtly.

'It's almost done,' the waiter said, his mouth dry. 'But don't get into it with Ned, stranger. He's good with that gun.'

'Go get the steak,' Bastian told him.

The waiter left the room and the fellow named Ned took a measured stance facing Bastian.

'I think you're all smoke and mirrors, Preacher. I reckon I can teach you a lesson about how to treat other folks. Stand up, by Jesus!'

Bastian couldn't believe it. This was why he hated being recognized anywhere he went. He took another small swig of the beer, and rose slowly.

'You don't really want this, do you, boy?'

'This is your last day on Earth, Preacher!' The young man's cheeks were a bit flushed.

In that moment, though, the waiter returned with a plate of food for Bastian. He saw what was happening, and stopped.

'Come on over and put it down here,' Bastian told him. 'I don't want it to get cold.'

The waiter followed orders, and retreated to the far side of the room quickly.

'OK, smart guy. You'll never taste that steak,' Ned said harshly. Then he went for the old Remington revolver at his hip.

But in that same instant, Bastian's

right hand drew the Colt on his belly so fast the eye couldn't follow, and suddenly the revolver was leveled at Ned's heart, while the young man's gun was still clearing its holster.

The challenger stopped halfway through the draw, and saw what had happened. His face revealed curious shock as he hesitated, then lowered the gun back into its resting place.

'Holy Jesus!' he muttered, expecting to be shot dead at any moment. The waiter whistled through his teeth. It was his first encounter with the Preacher.

In the following seconds, Bastian's Colt barked out savagely three times, tearing the fellow's hat off his head, cutting a leather strap that held his holster to his right thigh, and then severing the holster from its mooring at his gunbelt. The holster dropped to the floor with the revolver still in it, clattering loudly there in the echoes of the thunderous gunfire.

The young cowhand didn't look down at the gun on the floor. He felt a slight trembling begin inside him as he stood and waited.

But Bastian smoothly slid the Colt back into its special holster, sat down to his steak, and picked up a fork and knife. Gunsmoke was still hanging over the table. He didn't look up again at the other man.

'Leave the gun when you go.'

Then he was cutting off a piece of steak.

The fellow called Ned and the waiter exchanged stunned looks, then Ned was hurrying unsteadily out the door. The waiter walked over to Bastian warily.

'How did you do that? Who are you?'

'A man trying to eat a steak,' Bastian replied through the chewing. 'Now bring me another glass of that weak beer. This made me thirsty.'

The waiter nodded wide-eyed. 'Yes, sir.' In a tight voice. 'Anything you say, mister. Anything you say.'

★ ★ ★

The next morning was overcast in Medicine Bend, creating an appropriate mood for the three funerals that were held beginning at sunup at the local cemetery. The town buried Eli St Clair first, with a small ceremony led by Ethan Purvis. The hotel clerk whom Sweet Daddy had shot was put in the ground next, and then it was time for Jonah's grandfather. Jonah stood at the grave site with Purvis beside him and a few townsfolk who knew the old gentleman. A damp wind gusted over the proceedings as a local clergyman, dressed much like Luther Bastian, said a few words over the grave.

'And he saw a new Heaven and a new Earth, for the former Heaven and Earth had passed into oblivion, and also the sea was no more. He also saw the city, the New Jerusalem, coming down out of Heaven from God. And with that he heard a loud voice from the throne say, 'Look, the home of God is with humankind, and He will reside with them, and they will be His people.

And God himself will wipe out every tear from their eyes, and death will be no more, neither will mourning nor outcry nor pain be any more; the things of grief and sadness are passed away and gone for ever.''

Jonah stood there bravely, his blue eyes filled with tears.

'It's all right to cry,' Purvis whispered to him.

Jonah nodded and wiped at an eye as the casket of his grandfather was lowered into the ground.

'Ashes to ashes, dust to dust. Jeremiah Spencer now goes to claim his Great Reward. Let us pray.'

The voice droned on for the next several minutes as memories of Jonah's grandfather crowded through the boy's head. At last it was over.

'Come on, let's get home,' Purvis told the boy. 'My business for the day isn't finished yet.'

Jonah knew to what Purvis was referring. He had an appointment with Simon Gabriel at the hotel at noon.

Jonah and Purvis didn't talk all the way back to the mayor's house. Purvis knew that Jonah didn't want to talk about the Gabriel gang, or admit that Purvis was buying them off today, to get rid of them. In fact, Jonah hadn't spoken a word about last evening's dangerous episode from the moment Purvis discovered him as he returned from the saloon. He now left Jonah with his wife for a light lunch, while he walked down to the Mary Lou to meet with Gabriel.

The wind had died down and the sky was clearing in places when Purvis arrived at the hotel. There was a large suite and several rooms on the top floor, all occupied by Gabriel's people, and Purvis found the boss in the suite, packing a bedroll for his mount's irons. When he invited Purvis in he was in shirtsleeves and vest, with the bright kerchief at his throat. The scar along his cheek shone rather boldly as he greeted Purvis.

'Well. I wondered if you'd show. Step inside, Mayor.'

Purvis went in tentatively. He had no

idea whether he would leave the room alive. Gabriel turned to face him and looked very dangerous, and he was. He was tough physically and mentally, and none of his subordinates would have considered challenging his authority or his gun. He had been called out by many, lawmen and outlaws alike, and had never lost a draw-down. He was a soulless man who, in his younger days, had occasionally shot an Indian or black man more or less for sport. But with maturity he had finally understood the foolishness of such behavior.

Across the big room, sprawled on a long sofa, Pedro Rueda watched but said nothing, as he sucked on a thin cigar. He was Gabriel's most trusted hireling. Gabriel noted the small leather bag Purvis was carrying.

'So. You have the money?'

Purvis shot a glance at Rueda. 'I have all I could get. I have close to four thousand dollars in here, Gabriel. That cleans me out and a lot of other respectable folks. That should be enough to see you to wherever you'd like to go.'

Gabriel's face sobered up, but not dramatically. 'Give me the bag. And sit down.'

Purvis turned the bag over to him and took a seat in an overstuffed chair near him. Gabriel dropped into another chair near by, opened the bag and began counting the money out. After a moment, he put the bag down and sat back on the chair.

'So. You thought you'd cheat a little on our agreement, heh, Mr Mayor?'

Purvis felt his stomach tighten. 'I'm not cheating. And we didn't have an agreement. I told you. I did the best I could. It's a reasonable offer, Gabriel. You've bled us dry. Now leave us alone. That's all we want.'

Gabriel grunted out a small laugh and turned to Rueda. 'What do you think, Pedro? Is this good enough? Or shall we stay till we've got what we asked for?'

'Let's get out of this stinkhole!' Rueda said irritably. 'I feel like I'm serving a sentence here, *por Dios*!'

Gabriel grinned in a relaxed way. He took his Colt Army revolver out and spun the cylinder.

'All right, we don't want to be seen as greedy. But what about Mr Mayor? He did renege a little here, didn't he?'

'He did what?' Rueda said, squinting his dark eyes.

'Never mind. The point is, does he deserve some kind of punishment for this breach of promise?'

Purvis rose, dry-mouthed. 'I brought you a lot of money, Gabriel. Now let me go in peace.'

'What do you think, Pedro?' Gabriel said lightly, examining the gun. 'We wouldn't want it to get around that he cheated us and we did nothing about it. Am I right?'

Rueda blew on the end of his cigar. 'Shoot him. What do I care?'

Gabriel smiled at Purvis. 'Did you hear that, Purvis? The Mexican wants to shoot you.'

'I'm leaving,' Purvis said sharply.

'Not without permission,' Gabriel

replied. He aimed the Colt at Purvis.

'I told you before. That's all we have,' Purvis said, his mouth clicking.

'Ask permission,' Gabriel said with a sudden coldness.

Purvis glared at him, then licked his dry lips. 'OK. May I have permission to leave?'

Gabriel smiled again, and put the gun away. 'That's better. Sure, get out of here, Mr Mayor. I'm tired of looking at your yellow belly.'

Purvis didn't wait for a second invitation. He turned and quickly left the room. As he headed for the stairs he could hear Gabriel and Rueda laughing at him, and a little whining sound came from his throat as he left the building.

He had been gone but a few minutes when Cuckoo Bobo and Big Thelma entered the big suite. Gabriel was looking the money over again.

'He came through?' Thelma asked immediately. She was dressed in a fancy skirt, blouse and vest, decorated with beads and spangles, and looked more like a circus performer than an outlaw. Her black-and-gold gunbelt hung at her waist, higher than most gunslingers carried their iron, and she looked ready to shoot at targets for applause.

'He came through,' Gabriel replied. 'He was a little short, but we've got traveling money here. I'll make a division later. I want to be clear of this dung-pit in an hour. Is Eddie ready to go?'

'He said he's been ready ever since we got here.' Bobo grinned behind his crossed eye. 'He's oiling up that Iver Johnson of his like it was a whore he just slept with.'

'It has treated him better than any *puta*, *sí*?' Rueda laughed from the sofa.

'Say, I been talking to Daddy,' Bobo went on. 'He says you told him he could stay over for a couple days, and meet you in Fort Repulse.'

'Yeah. One of these store owners has got a shipment of shirts and vests coming in that Daddy wants to see. That boy has an eye for good clothes. I said he could stay on.'

'If it's OK, Simon, I'll stay with him,' Bobo said. 'Give him somebody to ride with into the Territory. It ain't smart to ride alone.'

Gabriel frowned. 'Since when did you worry over Sweet Daddy, my loco friend? You got no business here.'

Bobo hesitated. Unknown to Gabriel, a hatred for Jonah Spencer had been simmering inside him since the boy shot him, and he had vague notions of what he might do to make himself feel better about it. He couldn't decide whether to actually shoot the boy, or just make him wish he was dead for a while.

'Oh, I just thought I might take me another shot at that Jenkins girl before I ride out,' he lied, not wanting Gabriel to know his real plans. 'Collect a kind of going-away present, if you follow me.'

Thelma shook her head. 'Bobo always was an oversexed little head-case,' she offered openly and without fear of his reaction.

Bobo glared at her. 'Wish you'd seen her first, Thelma?' he growled.

Thelma shook her head. 'Nice try, Cuckoo boy. Everybody knows I like the menfolks. Of course, they got to be big. Not some shrimp like you, dearie.'

Bobo's face got red. He started to hurl a reply, but Gabriel intervened.

'All right, you two. You can stay with Daddy, Bobo. But be in Fort Repulse in a week. I'll be making big plans there. And I'll need all of you with me.'

Bobo gave one last blistering look at Thelma. 'OK, Simon. I'll be there.'

When he was gone, Gabriel turned to Thelma. 'You got that boy in a real bad mood. I pity the local that gives him any trouble in the next couple of days.'

'Well,' Rueda commented, 'nobody in this scared little town is likely to give him or Daddy any trouble now, *verdad*?'

Gabriel started to agree, but for some unaccountable reason, he got a brief bad feeling about voicing his concurrence.

'They'll be all right,' he said noncommitally. 'Let's get ready to ride out of here.'

4

Kiowa Junction was not as big as Medicine Bend. It was under the jurisdiction of federal marshals, but the town had never seen one. It lay close by the route that Simon Gabriel would take to Fort Repulse.

It was also the home of Maggie Spencer, the young aunt of Jonah.

Maggie had been raised in Medicine Bend, along with her brother who was Jonah's father, now deceased. Margaret Spencer had learned nursing in her late teens, and moved to the Territory where she figured her skills could help those more in need of them. Dr Avery Sumner had established a small clinic at Kiowa Junction, where settlers and also Indians came for treatment of various ills, from broken legs to tuberculosis, and he had been very happy to receive Maggie's help for a very modest salary.

Jonah was just a few months old when Maggie left, and he had no memory of ever seeing her. Before his parents could tell him much about her, they both contracted diphtheria and succumbed to it, leaving Jonah with Maggie's father, Jeremiah Spencer. When she heard of Jonah's parents' deaths, she fought guilt for a long time, thinking she might have made a difference if she had been there. She asked her father to send Jonah to her, but Jeremiah thought the disruption in the boy's life at the tender age of six would be too great for him. But recently, just a few days ago, she had received a wire from Mayor Purvis, telling of Jeremiah's death, and suggesting that she seemed an appropriate person to take custody of the boy. Also, unless Purvis heard from her to the contrary, Purvis would send Jonah to her as soon as transport could be arranged for him.

Maggie was elated with the prospect of having Jonah with her: her brother's son and her closest relative. Now, on a sunny afternoon, when Simon Gabriel was riding out from Medicine Bend toward the Territory, she received a second wire. This one warned her that Gabriel was headed her way, and that his gang was very dangerous.

Maggie stood in the reception area of the doctor's office with the message in her hand. The last patient of the day had departed, and she and the doctor were alone.

'Who is Simon Gabriel?' she asked rhetorically. 'And why does Purvis think I have to be concerned about him?'

Dr Sumner was standing in the doorway to his examination room. He was a middle-aged man with balding hair and eyeglasses on the end of his nose. He wore a white medical coat and a stethoscope.

'I've heard the name, Maggie,' he said. 'Gabriel is wanted in the Territory for bank and stage hold-ups. And murder.' He smiled wanly. 'Purvis probably had some trouble with him, and wants us to keep out of his way, that's all. These people never bother doctors, though.'

Maggie's pretty face revealed a mild concern. She was wearing a white uniform over a trim but full figure, and her dark hair was caught up in a bun behind her head. Her eyes were a soft, subtropical green, and sometimes they changed, chameleon-like, to a hazel hue. She was attractive to the men she met, but had lately lost a two-years fiancé when he became caught in a rare snowstorm and froze to death mounted on his horse.

'We don't have any law here,' she said after a long moment. 'I haven't seen a marshal since I came here almost ten years ago.'

'Medicine Bend has no marshal either,' the doctor reminded her. 'And that town apparently survived Gabriel.'

Maggie sat down on a nearby bench and dropped the telegraph message to her lap. 'Even so. I hope Purvis doesn't send Jonah here until Gabriel is gone.'

The doctor studied her face. 'Maggie, you're almost thirty now, aren't you?'

She looked up at him curiously. 'For someone pushing sixty, you make that sound a bit aged, Doctor.' She gave him a lovely smile.

He went and sat beside her, removing the spectacles. 'You've hardly left your rooms since your brother Aaron died, except to come here to the clinic. This isn't much of a life for a young woman, Maggie. Maybe you should leave Kiowa Junction. You could get a good job in Austin, or Abilene. And you might meet some young men in a bigger place. The only eligible bachelors hereabouts are a couple of farmers who couldn't tie their own shoelaces without supervision.'

'You need me here, Doctor. Your patients need me.'

'Yes, but what do you need? You're entitled to a life just as much as any patient who walks in here.'

'When Jonah gets here I'll have a life,' she argued.

'That's not what I'm talking about,' he said. 'A woman needs a man, Maggie.' He rose. 'Just give it some thought.'

She rose, too, and embraced him warmly. 'You're a good guy, Doctor.

Too bad you lost Abbie. You need a life, too.'

He placed a kiss on her cheek. She was like a daughter to him. 'I've had a life, Maggie. But you haven't.'

'Jonah will give me everything I need,' she assured him. 'Really. I'm looking forward very much to his arrival.'

'You're a stubborn girl,' he told her. And the conversation was over.

* * *

It was just two hours after Simon Gabriel had ridden out of town when Luther Bastian arrived in Medicine Bend on his black stallion.

He had never been there before. He looked around disdainfully as he rode down Main Street to Ethan Purvis's house, and dismounted there. The weather had warmed up, so he had discarded the dark suit coat in favor of his black vest over a plain gray shirt. Because of this, he had had to remove the specially hand-made shoulder holster with its deadly

93

Meriden pocket revolver. He liked to keep its presence as private as possible. But the custom-altered Colt Peacemaker in its break-away holster was even more obvious and dangerous-looking without the jacket. The three guns on his stallion's irons were seldom used by him, but were available if needed.

He was met at Purvis's door by the mayor's wife, who looked him over warily.

'Yes?'

'I'm here to see the mayor,' Bastian told her without fanfare, standing tall and ominous outside the doorway.

'Are you with them?' she asked with fear in her voice.

'I'm not with anybody,' he said. 'Is he here?'

She hesitated. 'Just a moment.'

When Purvis arrived Bastian was still standing outside. Purvis glanced at the Colt on Bastian's gunbelt.

'Can I help you, mister?'

'Brett Mallory sent me. About St Clair.'

Purvis's face softened. 'Oh. You're a Ranger?'

'No. You might say I'm here on hire. I was sent for to go after Gabriel and his men.'

Purvis's eyes narrowed. 'Ah. You're one of them. But there's no bounties on Gabriel's people.'

'Let me worry about the bounties,' Bastian said. 'Mind if we talk inside?'

'Oh, sure. Excuse my manners.' Purvis stepped aside for Bastian. 'Find yourself a chair.'

When they were seated Purvis folded his hands on the kitchen table that stood between them.

'You're too late, anyway. Gabriel rode off earlier today. We think for the Territory. Fort Repulse was mentioned.'

Bastian muttered something under his breath.

'Say, would you be the Preacher?'

Bastian scowled at him. 'Some flea-brains have called me that. The name is Bastian. Luther Bastian.'

Purvis nodded solemnly. 'Pleasure to

meet you, Bastian. I hope the stories about you are false.' He gave a half-smile.

'They are,' Bastian said coolly. 'How long ago did Gabriel leave?'

'Oh, I'd say mid-afternoon. But two of his gang stayed behind. I think for a day or two.'

Bastian felt better. 'Which ones?'

'Well, that crazy one stayed. Bobo, his name is.' Purvis rubbed a hand across his mouth. 'I think that lunatic has plans to harm Jonah, the damn snake.'

'Who's Jonah?'

'An orphan boy in my custody. We're trying to find a way to get him to his aunt in the Territory.'

Bastian showed no interest. 'And the other man?'

'The one they call Daddy. He's French or something. I hear he recites sonnets and picks wild flowers. An odd bird. But they all are.'

'Are they at the hotel?'

Purvis nodded. 'Last I heard. Are you going after them?'

Before Bastian could reply Jonah came into the kitchen from the stable, where he had been feeding Purvis's two carriage horses. But he was sleeping in the house now, in a cot Purvis had erected for him, because of Bobo. Jonah stopped inside the doorway and stared at Bastian.

'Oh. I thought you was alone.'

'Come on in, Jonah,' Purvis told him. He turned to Bastian. 'This is the boy I mentioned to you.'

Bastian glanced at Jonah abstractedly. 'Right. Listen, I might take a walk down to the hotel, if I can leave my mount with you?'

'Of course,' Purvis said.

'Are you a lawman?' Jonah asked bluntly.

Bastian rose from his chair. 'Do you see a badge, kid?' he responded impatiently. Then, to Purvis: 'I'll be back for the stallion.' He turned and left the house. Jonah and Purvis stared after him for a moment.

'That's the Preacher, boy,' Purvis

explained. 'A very dangerous bounty hunter. Too bad he wasn't here a few days ago.'

'The Preacher!' Jonah exclaimed. 'Gramps told me about him. He back-shoots wanted men and then reads scripture over them.'

Purvis grunted out a laugh. 'I suspect those stories aren't true, Jonah. He isn't that kind of man. I can tell from his eyes.'

'Is he going to kill Bobo and that other one?'

Purvis couldn't tell the boy how much he hoped so. 'I reckon we'll have to wait and see, Jonah,' he said quietly. 'We'll just wait and see.'

★   ★   ★

It was a short walk to the Mary Lou Hotel. It was early evening and there was plenty of light in the western sky, where ribbons of pastel hues had begun to form just above the horizon, out on the plains. Bastian wore only the vest and the Colt, but still gave off an aura of trouble. He found a clerk behind the small registration desk, and signed in as John Smith.

'Do you have any luggage, sir?' asked the replacement for the man Daddy had shot recently: a young, red-haired fellow wearing a green visor.

'I'll bring some stuff in later,' Bastian told him. 'Say, I hear a couple friends of mine are staying here. Bobo and Rochambert.'

The clerk's face went a bit pale. 'Why, yes. They'll be here for another day or so. They're on the top floor, in adjacent rooms.'

Bastian nodded. 'Are they in?'

'I don't think so. The one they call Daddy went over to Burley's General Store, I think. They were obtaining some merchandise he was interested in. And I'd guess that Bobo is over at the Prairie Schooner. That's a saloon.'

Bastian nodded. 'I'll find them. And if they should return, don't mention I was asking. I want to surprise them.'

The clerk nodded, and Bastian left, heading for the general store, which was just down the street. When he arrived there, only a clerk, Sweet Daddy and a woman shopper were present. Bastian's riding spurs betrayed his presence, but nobody took any notice except the woman, who was looking at bolts of cloth at a table set against a far wall. She stopped and stared at Bastian for just a short moment, then turned and, making a wide circuit around him, left the store.

The clerk, behind a short counter, heard the door close, looked up, and made a sound in his throat.

'Well. I wonder what that was all about?' He looked Bastian over. 'I'll be right with you, sir.'

Daddy was examining a brocaded shirt, and had decided to buy it. He had also put several other items aside for possible purchase. Bobo had shown no interest in coming here with him, but was very content to spend this extra time in town at the Prairie Schooner.

Daddy glanced now at the newcomer. When he saw that Bastian's attention was fastened on himself, he narrowed his brow with curiosity.

'Are you Daddy Rochambert?' Bastian said from across the room.

Daddy put the shirt down and looked him over. 'My friends call me Sweet Daddy,' he said with a pleasant smile. 'My, what a handsome one to ask! You aren't the Cheyenne Kid, are you? I heard he was in this area.'

'I killed the Kid,' Bastian said evenly.

Daddy's brow furrowed. 'Killed him? What in the world for?'

'He had a bounty on his head,' Bastian said. 'Just like you, Daddy.'

Daddy just stood there letting all that make sense to him, then he burst out laughing. 'You're here to kill me?'

'Now, wait a minute, boys,' the store clerk broke in. 'This is no place for that. Take your argument elsewhere.'

'Yes, I came here to kill you,' Bastian said.

Daddy faced him casually. 'I don't

know where you came from, handsome.
But you'd better head right back there.
You can't beat me. I'm the fastest draw
in five states.'

'Gentlemen!' the clerk pleaded.

'I know your reputation,' Bastian
said. 'But I suggest you defend yourself,
Frenchie. You should have left town
with Gabriel.'

Daddy's dark-blue eyes darkened
even more as he felt the insult of
Bastian's jibe.

'Well. I'd rather have a drink with
you. But if you want to die, fine. I'll
oblige you.'

When Daddy went for the Smith &
Wesson .32 on his left hip, it was as if
the gun had been ready in his hand all
the time. There was no way to see the
motion that had put it there. The gun
fired twice in rapid succession before
Bastian got a shot off.

But Bastian had seen the move in
Daddy's eyes, and had already dropped
into a low crouch as the other man's
revolver roared in the room. Daddy's

first shot, therefore, only tore a hole in Bastian's gray shirt as it went on to smash a large jar of hard candies on a shelf behind him. Daddy's second shot grazed Bastian's neck on the right side, just missing his jugular, and then Bastian's only retort ripped through Daddy's heart like a hot iron.

Daddy slammed up against the counter as the clerk screamed loudly. The gunman just stood there, staring unbelievingly at Bastian, not understanding what could have gone wrong. His gun fired a third time, into the floor, then he slumped into a sitting position, eyes still open in the rictus of death.

Bastian rose to his full height, twirled the Colt over twice in his hand, and nestled it back into its holster. Gunsmoke hung heavy in the room.

'He really was the fastest gun in five states,' Bastian commented to himself as he placed a kerchief on his wound. Then he left the store, the clerk still staring after him, open-mouthed.

5

The sun was just setting on a distant hill when Gabriel and his men stopped for the night. Eddie had started a camp-fire and Thelma was frying up some tinned beef to go with coffee and corn dodgers. Rueda had watered and picketed the horses, and now returned to the fire where Gabriel sat on his saddle poking at the fire with a stick.

'I shouldn't have let Daddy stay on there,' he was grumbling. 'He's the only one of us that can cook.'

Big Thelma gave him a look, and stirred the meat in the pan. 'Hey. Did I ever claim any culinary skill? You hired me because I can shoot, Simon.'

'Oh, I know. It's not on you. It's just that I hate it when we have to make camp like this. I've gotten soft, I guess. I like the comfort of a town.'

'That will be the day.' Eddie grinned.

'When you go soft, boss. Say, don't fry that beef too crisp, woman.'

'Woman?' Thelma said acidly.

Eddie absorbed her dark look and threw a chunk of wood on the fire. Bright sparks rose into a growing blackness. He considered it bad luck to have a woman with them. He turned to Gabriel.

'This should be our only night in the open. Tomorrow we hit Kiowa Junction. It's small, but I think there might be a rooming-house there. And a saloon. We could rest up a couple days before riding on to Fort Repulse.'

Gabriel nodded. 'I planned on that. There's a backwoods clinic there, too, and I've got a boil on my neck I need looked at.'

'I've got a corn on my left foot, too. Maybe the doctor there can fix that up.' Eddie was a resolute complainer of everything, and that trait irritated Gabriel rather regularly.

'You had that corn when I hired you,' Gabriel said sourly. 'Stand still while I shoot that toe off and you'll be cured.'

Rueda laughed in his throat and Eddie gave Gabriel a sour look.

'Very funny, Simon. I just hope you get one some day.'

'If I do I won't talk about it all the time,' Gabriel grunted. 'Now. Let's talk business while that beef is frying.' The meat was beginning to sizzle in the pan now, and Thelma was doing more stirring, squatting by the fire. 'We have the bank in Fort Repulse. And we have a stage line that goes right through there. Neither one has been hit lately, and I think they're both ripe for plucking.'

Eddie grinned. 'Now you're talking. I say we take both of them. Then ride out further east. The whole Territory is rich nowadays, since all the new settlers arrived. We should never have left. It's like one big candy store.'

'There is hardly any law in the Territory,' Rueda observed. He was leaning against a nearby sapling. 'What there is, we can out-gun.'

'If those two slackers we left behind decide to get down to business again,'

Eddie complained in a dour tone. 'I think you cut that Daddy too much slack, Simon. He's not dependable.'

' 'Not dependable?' ' Thelma retorted, her thick face clouding over. 'He's twice as valuable to this crew as you, Rip Van Winkle!' She was referring to his capture while asleep under a tree.

Eddie's face went straight-lined. 'Maybe you miss what he can do for you, Thelma. Especially since no other man will look at you.'

In the next instant Thelma threw the contents of the frying-pan on to Eddie. The beef and grease hit him squarely in the face.

Eddie yelled loudly as the grease burned at his flesh, just missing his eyes. He tore his kerchief off and began rubbing at his cheeks and forehead; the other three just stood, unmoving. After a moment he threw the kerchief down, revealing some red and blistering spots on his face.

'Ha!' Rueda exclaimed, unbelieving.

Eddie drew the Iver Johnson at his

side, but then saw Thelma's revolver already aimed at his chest.

'Go ahead, you defamer,' she spat out. 'We'll both go down.'

Gabriel rose to his feet. 'I should shoot you both. Put those damn guns away.'

They just stood across the fire from each other, one staring hard at the other.

Finally, Eddie glanced at Gabriel.

'Look what she did to me! Do you expect me to take this?' His flesh still burned hotly.

'Now you've really got something to see the doctor about in Kiowa Junction,' Gabriel said without inflection. 'Now, I mean it. Both of you. Put them away or I'll finish it.' He put his right hand out over his gun.

Thelma holstered her gun first. Then Eddie followed, reluctantly.

'Good,' Gabriel muttered, shaking his head. 'I'll put some bear grease on those burns so you can sleep tonight, Eddie. And listen. You did insult her. Now call it quits. Do you both hear me?'

Eddie nodded silently. Thelma muttered, 'Yes.'

Gabriel sighed, and sat back down beside the fire. 'Thelma, get some more beef out. Eddie, go find some more firewood. Pedro, get Eddie some of that bear lard we got stored on Thelma's mount. And — I never thought I'd be saying this, but I can't wait till Bobo and Daddy rejoin us in Fort Repulse.

'They might actually lend some stability to this crazy outfit I put together.'

★   ★   ★

At the Prairie Schooner saloon, Henry Bobo had drunk some of the establishment's best liquor, driven most other patrons away, and bored the scared bartender with stories about his escapades in the Indian Territory. Now the sun was down and he was thinking about joining Sweet Daddy at the hotel for an evening meal.

But then Burley's store clerk came in, face flushed, out of breath.

'Somebody go for the mayor. That one they call Daddy was shot and killed in my store. Bartender, give me a double whiskey.'

Bobo rose slowly, his face forming a deep scowl. He went over to the clerk and grabbed him by the shirt front.

'What the hell are you doing? Coming in here and lying like that? Nobody could kill Daddy!'

'I'm telling you,' the clerk insisted. 'It was right in my store. The boy was looking at shirts. Then this man came in. Black vest, black hat. He killed your friend. With one shot. That's all it took. Just one shot. Somebody come and get him, for God's sake!'

Bobo released his hold on the clerk and shoved him away so hard the fellow slammed into the bar and almost fell.

'That's a damn lie!' Bobo said loudly. Then he stormed from the saloon and headed on foot to the store.

When he arrived there he found

Daddy still in the same position as Bastian had left him: sitting against the store counter, eyes open, shock on his lifeless face. A crimson stain had spread across his chest.

Bobo just stared down at him as if witnessing a hallucination. Bobo himself was good with a gun, but he had considered Daddy unkillable. And the description given by the clerk made the killer sound like a bounty hunter whom some called the Preacher.

Bobo got himself under control. He had to accept it. Daddy was dead, and he, Bobo, was here in this rat-hole of a town with a deadly hunter of men.

He bent down, ransacked Daddy's pockets and found some gold pieces. He pocketed them, then found a gold watch and slid that also into a pocket. He leaned against the counter. He had been going to pay the boy Jonah a little visit before they left. Maybe cut him up, or bust some bones. Something the kid could live with for a long time, to remember Bobo by.

But now that had to go on a back burner. He had to decide whether to run and hope to keep ahead of Daddy's killer, or ambush and back-shoot him right here and get it over with. He chose the latter.

But he had to find the Preacher first. He would probably be at the hotel or maybe at the mayor's place. He would find the Preacher before the Preacher found him. Of course, that would require planning. He would hide out during the day, keeping out of sight, hoping the bounty hunter wouldn't guess his whereabouts. Then he would track his movements at night, and catch him where he would least expect trouble. If he did it right it would be like shooting fish in a barrel.

Also, that would mean giving up his room at the hotel. And his drinking at the Schooner. He couldn't appear any place where the bounty man would look for him. But he had to make one more visit to the saloon.

He walked back down there warily,

watching doorways and alleys. He didn't enter the saloon until he had satisfied himself from outside that Bastian wasn't there, waiting for him. It was dark outside now and he almost hoped to see Bastian inside. He would wait for him to leave and back-shoot him from an alleyway.

But Bastian wasn't there. Bobo walked in past several customers who regarded him with dark looks. He went over to the bartender, who was arranging shelves behind the bar.

'Hey. Barkeep.'

The other man turned reluctantly at the sound of his voice. 'Oh, Mr Bobo. I'm surprised to see you back here.'

Bobo frowned. 'Surprised? What the hell are you saying?'

The barkeep's face blanched. 'No offense. I just meant, with your friend lying dead at the store.'

'That was that yellow weasel bounty hunter that done that.'

'Somebody said it was Luther Bastian.'

'Is that his name? Well, he must have

gone in there with his gun already out and ready for murder. He'd never outdraw Daddy.'

'I wouldn't know,' the bartender said quietly. Secretly, he felt a little safer and bolder with Bobo's cohort gone.

'Well, now he'll be coming after me,' Bobo said, lowering his voice. 'That damn maggot! And that brings me to you.'

'Huh?'

'I want to be advised if he comes in here,' Bobo said conspiratorially, his crossed eye looking psychotic. 'Do you read me clear, mister?'

The bartender licked dry lips. 'Sure. I can do that. Where can I reach you?'

Bobo hadn't thought that far ahead. He looked down for a moment.

'The Jenkins girl.' He referred to the girl he had forced himself on twice during his stay at Medicine Bend. 'If Bastian comes in here, you go tell her. Or send that kid that works for you. I'll fix it up with her. She's scared to death of me.'

'Sure, Bobo. The Jenkins girl.'

Bobo drew the Tranter at his hip and placed its muzzle carefully on the bridge of the barkeep's nose.

'If I find out you failed me, I'll blow your liver out through your ribs. Got it?'

The barman nodded desperately. 'I understand. Will you be staying there, then?'

Bobo's face looked ferocious for a moment. 'If your brains was dynamite, you couldn't blow the top of your head off. Just do what I told you.'

The barkeep nodded again. 'You can count on me,' he said somberly.

★　★　★

Bastian had looked for Bobo at the hotel after the encounter with Sweet Daddy, and not finding him there he had walked back to the mayor's house. Purvis couldn't see Bastian's wound when he invited him back in, as it was hidden by Bastian's neckerchief. Jonah was there, sitting at the kitchen table,

115

and Bastian didn't insist on the boy's leaving.

'Didn't expect you back so soon,' Purvis said when they were all seated. 'Can I get you a cup of coffee?'

Bastian shook his head, and removed his black Stetson-type hat, revealing very dark long hair. Behind the stern countenance he was a rather handsome man.

'I'll be eating a late supper at the hotel.'

'I'd be careful at the hotel,' Purvis advised. 'That Rochambert fellow was seen there earlier.'

'He's dead,' Bastian said.

'Dead?' Purvis exclaimed. 'Do you mean . . . ?'

'I mean that's one down out of six,' Bastian said.

In that moment a look of stunned pleasure etched itself on to Jonah's young face, and a feeling of hero-worship burgeoned inside him such as he had never felt before.

'You killed Daddy? And you're going after the others?' he asked in awe.

Bastian looked over at him. 'Why don't you go milk a cow or something, kid?'

Purvis smiled. 'I figure he has the right to be here. He almost killed Bobo himself, you know.'

Bastian regarded Jonah more studiedly. 'You got grit, kid. But this stuff isn't for a tadpole like you.' He touched the bandanna and blood came away on his hand.

'Good lord! You're shot,' Purvis said loudly.

Jonah rose quickly, and went around the table and examined the bloody cloth.

'This needs to be cleaned, Mayor. Here, I'll take it off.'

Bastian made as though to stop him, but then let him remove the cloth. Purvis was over there now, too.

'Go get us some hot water, Jonah. And there's gauze and tape in the medicine cabinet.'

'This isn't necessary,' Bastian protested.

'It is while you're in this house,' Purvis answered.

A few minutes later Bastian's shallow wound was bandaged, and Jonah had found a yellow bandanna to replace the black one. Bastian allowed him to put it on him, watching him as the boy worked.

'You've got some know-how, kid.'

'I took care of my grandfather,' Jonah said proudly.

'The boy has just lost him,' Purvis told Bastian. 'We're trying to get him to his aunt in the Territory.'

Jonah was finished. He went to resume his seat at the table and Bastian looked over at him.

'Sorry about your loss, boy. But I'd guess you'll do just fine.'

Jonah was looking at Bastian as if he were a knight on a white horse.

'I'm mighty proud to meet you, Mr Bastian. You're kind of like a Ranger, aren't you?'

Bastian smiled and leaned back on his chair, looking over at Purvis.

'Bobo will know by now what happened. He might run, but I doubt he has the sense. He'll try to kill me.'

Jonah's eyes were big, but he said nothing.

'He won't give you a fair fight,' Purvis said.

'I know. I'll watch my back. I was hoping you might let me keep the stallion here till I'm finished with this. Feed him and stable him. I can pay.'

'Of course we'll take care of him. And I don't run a business here. His board and care are on the house.'

'I'll feed him,' Jonah said brightly.

Bastian nodded. 'Much obliged. To both of you.'

'Why don't you sleep here?' Purvis suggested. 'The hotel room could prove a bit insecure.'

'No, I want him to find me,' Bastian said. 'I sleep light. There's no way he could surprise me in bed.'

'Your choice,' Purvis said. 'Look, the missus could fix you some leftovers. She's upstairs in her sewing room.'

'I'll pass on that, too,' Bastian told him. 'I might find out something at the

119

hotel dining room.' He rose. 'You've been good to me, Mayor. I'm not used to that.'

'Any enemy of Gabriel is a friend of mine.' Purvis grinned.

'If things go well I'll be back for the stallion. If they don't, he's yours.'

'You'll be back, Mr Bastian,' Jonah said. 'You got four more to go after this crazy one.'

Bastian's face softened when he responded. 'That's true, kid,' he said. 'And thanks for the bandanna.'

'I like it,' Jonah told him. 'All that black made you look unhappy.'

That comment earned a rare smile from Bastian. 'You know, you might be right. I'll give it a fair trial.'

That left Jonah beaming as Bastian left, heading for the hotel.

When Bastian arrived back at the hotel he headed for the dining room, but the clerk at the desk stopped him.

'Oh, Mr Smith. Your friend Mr Bobo was asking about you earlier. Sorry you missed him. I think he was all shook up about his friend. Oh, that's right. You knew him, too. Did you hear about the shooting? Right over at the general store.'

'Yes, I heard,' Bastian said. 'Too bad. But I didn't know him that well. If Mr Bobo returns, feel free to tell him I'm in the dining room.'

'Of course. I hear they have a nice little rib steak tonight. I hope you enjoy your meal.'

Bobo didn't show during Bastian's meal. Bastian sat facing the lobby and ate six eggs and fried potatoes hungrily. He was always hungry while on the hunt. He spotted his reflection in a pane of glass across the room, and saw the yellow kerchief at his neck, which replaced his black lariat tie. With that and the gray-blue shirt he now affected a different look. It bothered him for a moment, but when he looked again, something about it appealed to him. The different look not only softened his exterior, it seemed to make him feel different inside. Which struck him as a bit absurd.

Maybe it had to do with Purvis, who had shown a paid killer kindness. And the innocence of the boy, who had put the bandanna on him.

Bastian decided he had had a big enough day, so he retired to his room shortly after his evening meal. He didn't bother to check Bobo's hotel room on the top floor, or any of those occupied by the Gabriel gang. He knew that Bobo wouldn't be at the hotel. The wild-acting gunman wouldn't invite a face-down with Bastian. He would seek a much safer way to kill him.

Before Bastian went to bed, though, he took a .44 cartridge from his gunbelt and balanced it on the inside doorknob after he had closed the room door. If the knob were turned in the night, to open the door, the lead-and-brass cartridge would fall to the wooden floor and clatter loudly there, waking Bastian. He had used the device before, and it had saved his life on at least one occasion.

That night the bullet never fell.

Cuckoo Bobo had no intention of trying to murder Bastian in his sleep. It was too risky a proposition with a man like the Preacher. He had hoped that Bastian would go looking for him at the Schooner that night, and had made careful plans for Bastian's demise if that happened. There was a nice little alley-way on the way to the hotel from the saloon that Bastian would have to walk right past, and Bobo would have been hidden in deep shadow there. Of course, that could still happen the following night. In the meantime, Bobo arranged in his head several other possibilities. All involving ambush. A situation where Bastian would die with his gun in its holster.

All this required considerable cour-age on the part of Bobo, a man who was no match for Bastian in a face-down, and he knew it. But if he could kill this murderer for money, even before Gabriel knew of his danger to the gang,

Bobo would be a small hero to Gabriel, and would rise in Gabriel's esteem. This was Bobo's big chance to show his value to Gabriel and the gang, and he was not going to let it pass.

The following day, therefore, while Bastian was looking for him, Bobo went into hiding at the Jenkins house, where he had satisfied himself with the girl there. It was the only safe place where Bastian would never look for him. Then, when night came, Bobo would find his chance. Or, perhaps, even before.

When Bastian rose that morning he felt confident that he would locate Bobo that day and a third of his assignment would be finished. Then he would be riding off to the Territory to track down the others.

He checked out Bobo's room first, just to make sure he wasn't there. He also checked Daddy's room and the rest of the floor, including the suite where Gabriel had holed up. As he had figured, they were all vacant. After a hot cup of coffee in the dining room he walked down to the town hostelry and confirmed that Bobo's mount was still there.

At mid-morning he entered the Prairie Schooner saloon.

There were just two patrons present at that hour, standing at the bar. They were talking in low tones with the bartender as Bastian walked in, and all three turned to stare at him as his riding spurs caught their attention. The bartender sucked his breath in.

'The Preacher. That's the Preacher. He'll be looking for Bobo.'

Bastian couldn't make out what he was saying. He walked over and leaned on the bar beside the two men.

'I'll take a sarsaparilla,' he said, ordering a non-alcoholic substitute for whiskey.

'Sure. Coming right up,' the bartender told him, giving the others a knowing look.

The two early drinkers were cowboys from a nearby ranch, and were considered to be troublemakers in the bunkhouse.

The taller one turned to Bastian.

'I understand you're the Preacher.'

Bastian looked him over. 'I'm Luther Bastian. If that's any of your business.'

The shorter one frowned. They both considered themselves good with guns.

'You're feeling a little juicy there, ain't you, Preacher? You ain't talking to no crazy, cross-eyed horse-thief now, you know.'

They laughed smugly between themselves. The bartender delivered Bastian's drink and he drank it down in one long swig. He had to deal with this a lot in saloons, when drinkers thought they were tougher than they really were. He tried to ignore them.

'Speaking of that, barkeep, has Mr Bobo been in here yet today?'

'Don't tell him nothing,' the stout one said sourly. 'He's a back-shooting killer for money, ain't he?'

The bartender looked scared. 'He ain't been in today at all.'

'Do you know where I might find him?' Bastian persisted.

'You heard my friend, bartender,' said the taller one. 'You keep out of it. You don't have to be no accessory to murder.'

Bastian sighed. 'Don't you boys have work to do at the ranch?'

'I don't know nothing,' the bartender said quickly.

'You ought to go somewhere else to drink,' the short cowboy said. 'Me and my friend, we don't like to drink with gunslingers.'

Bastian turned to them for the first time. 'You two got clabber for brains. I was leaving, anyway. Don't you know yet when to keep your mouths shut?' He threw some coins on to the bar.

'You telling us to shut up, mister?' the tall one said hostilely. He felt unjustified confidence in numbers, with their two guns to one. With a couple of beers in him he didn't understand that that made no difference whatever.

Bastian didn't want to kill anybody but Bobo. So he threw a hard left fist into the tall man's face, keeping his gunhand guarded. Under the dark clothing Bastian was well muscled, and the blow snapped the tall cowboy's nose as he staggered backward, slammed into his companion and took the short fellow to the floor with him. They both lay there dazed for a moment, blood running down the tall man's face. He grew a slow scowl.

'Why, you — ' He stupidly went for his gun, but what happened next saved his life.

Bobo appeared suddenly at the swing doors, glittery-eyed, Tranter revolver in hand, and wildly fired off a quick shot at Bastian.

The gun exploded raucously in the confines of the room, and what happened in the next few seconds occurred so blindingly fast that nobody could remember details later. Bastian had heard the swinging slatted doors as Bobo came through them. He had just started to react: turning, so that when the hot chunk of lead slugged him in the torso it was high in his left-side ribs instead of his back. As Bastian was slammed against the bar he was already drawing the Colt Peacemaker and fanning the hammer in lightning-fast motion. He hit Bobo in the stomach, the high chest, and the throat.

Bobo's crossed eyes widened as he crashed through the doors behind him with arms flung wide, splintering the slats as he disappeared outside. He hit the dirt out there, choking and coughing for a moment as his face turned a dull shade of blue, then he let out a last ragged breath and died there.

Bobo had violated his own rule to stay hidden in the daytime. He had forgotten to tell the bartender at the Schooner that he wouldn't be at the Jenkins place past sundown, and had made his way along back streets to the saloon. When he looked inside and saw Bastian there, with his back exposed, Bobo decided to let circumstances dictate his action.

It hadn't worked out for him.

In the saloon, with Bastian leaning

heavily against the bar, the two cowpokes were getting to their feet, their whole manner changed. The short one now spoke up.

'I'm getting to hell out of here. Come on.'

The tall one with the broken nose wiped some blood off his lower face, hesitated, and nodded his agreement.

'OK.'

They were gone a minute later. Outside, they paused over the corpse of Bobo for a moment, then saddled up and rode out.

Inside, Bastian felt under his vest and his hand came away, stained crimson. He turned to the stunned bartender.

'Get Purvis for me.'

The fellow knew better than to argue with him. While he was gone Bastian slumped on to a chair near by, feeling weak and dizzy. It took Purvis just ten minutes to arrive; he had the town's horse doctor with him, since there were no physicians in Medicine Bend. The vet drew two tables together and stripped off Bastian's vest and shirt. When his gunbelt was removed Bastian at first attempted to stop them, but then allowed the denuding.

'I told you to watch your back,' Purvis said, standing over the doctor's shoulder.

'It was the cowboys,' Bastian grunted out. 'I let them distract me.'

'Bobo is already at the mortician's with quarters on his eyes,' Purvis went on, with some satisfaction. Bastian flinched as the vet examined him.

'It's a through-and-through,' the man announced. 'But the lead broke one of your ribs. You'll have to have some taping.'

'That's fine,' Bastian said, feeling a little better.

'Say, you got other places here. Old scars. What kind of business are you in, mister?'

'Nothing interesting, Doc,' Bastian grunted out.

Less than an hour later Bastian was bandaged and taped up, and was being driven to Purvis's house in the mayor's carriage. Bastian now accepted the extra cot in a spare room and, with a little laudanum in him, slept the rest of the day.

When he opened his eyes at just after sunset Jonah was standing over him, wide-eyed.

'Oh. Mr Bastian, you're awake.'

Bastian focused on him. 'What's going on, kid? What are you doing here? Where's my gun?'

'It's right here.' Jonah smiled at him. 'On the chair over there. And your other ones are safe in the stable, too. All four of them.' This last was said with a bit of awe.

'They all have their functions,' Bastian said. He started to sit up, and cried out softly in pain. 'Damn that cross-eyed psycho,' Bastian grumbled.

Jonah grinned widely as Bastian lay back down. 'I knew he couldn't kill you. You're too good.'

Bastian gave him a narrow look. 'Don't you have chores to do, boy?'

'I came in to find out if you wanted anything. Coffee. Sassafras tea. The missus made some soup.'

'Not now,' Bastian said, grimacing as he moved on the cot. His face softened. 'But thanks for asking.'

'It's a pleasure and an honor, Mr Bastian. Well, I'll let you rest.'

Bastian studied the young face and wondered whether he had ever looked that innocent.

'I hope you get to join your aunt soon.'

'Oh. Thanks. Some days I forget I have to go. But I don't like it here any more. The mayor is trying to find someone to take me out there. I just have to be patient.'

'There's little more important in life,' Bastian told him. 'Where did you say the aunt lives?'

'In Kiowa Junction. In the Territory.'

'Hmmph. And that's where Gabriel was headed.'

Jonah's face changed. He hadn't put the two things together. 'Are you still going after Gabriel?'

Bastian saw the change in Jonah's face. 'As soon as I'm able. But, no. You can't ride with me. Forget it.'

'I wouldn't be any trouble. I can cook. Help make camp. Gramps taught me how to take care of myself. Please, Mr Bastian.'

Bastian's face clouded over. 'Get out of here, kid. That's a dead issue.'

Jonah looked as if he had been slapped in the face. After a moment he murmured, 'Yes, sir.'

Bastian watched him leave the room, feeling bad now. 'Damn kids,' he muttered.

Bastian slept the rest of that night, and began taking soup the next morning. By noon he had got up and donned a blue shirt that Purvis had found for him. When it came to putting the yellow bandanna back on, he hesitated, then replaced it around his neck. He left the gunbelt behind when he went to lunch downstairs with the others, and felt almost naked without it.

His ribcage hurt whenever he moved, and he realized it needed to heal. When he and Purvis went to sit on a front porch together after lunch Purvis broached the subject.

'It's going to take a while for that rib to heal.'

'It will be a few weeks before I have good function again. Fortunately, it's my left side. It shouldn't impair my draw at all.'

They were sitting together on a two-seat bench. 'You've done a marvelous job here, Luther. This whole town is indebted to you.'

'I appreciate the help you gave me. I owe you one.'

Purvis turned toward him. 'You don't have to go after those others. They're off in the Territory now. Where they came from. Let the federal marshals deal with them. You have to heal.'

Bastian looked over at him. 'I obligated myself on an oral agreement, Purvis. Brett Mallory wants to show the gunslingers of the world that they can't kill a Texas

Ranger and get away with it. He wants blood, Mayor. And I'm the guy that has to deliver it to him.'

'These are dangerous men, Luther. You'd have had a tough enough time with them if you'd stayed uninjured. As a friend, I'm suggesting you don't go. Tell Mallory to get somebody else to do his dirty work. You have a good reason to quit now.'

Bastian smiled at him. 'Look, Mr Mayor. There are probably a dozen US marshals to service the whole damned Territory, and fifty times that many bad guys for them to deal with. In the meantime, people like Gabriel will continue stealing, raping and killing until they're stopped. There's nobody available to stop him but me. That's just the way it is.'

Purvis sat back on the bench. 'Well, I guess you're going.'

'Yes. I'm going.'

Purvis paused. 'I reckon they'll pass through Kiowa Junction on their way east.'

'I suppose so.'

'You said you owe me one. Did you mean it?'

Bastian frowned at him. 'Now, wait a minute, Mayor. I've already told the kid I couldn't do that. God knows what trouble I might find on the trail between here and there. I don't want the responsibility. I'm not a damn nursemaid.'

'Jonah isn't a baby, Luther. And you're his only means of getting to Kiowa Junction in the near future. Why don't you give him the life he deserves? With his aunt, who will take him and love him?'

Bastian suddenly felt the kerchief around his neck that Jonah had put there. His hand went to it subconsciously.

'You ask a lot, Mayor.'

'I know.'

Bastian muttered an obscenity under his breath, then: 'I'll be riding out in a couple of days. Get the kid ready to go.'

Purvis let out a long breath. 'Thanks, Luther. You won't regret it.'

'I regret it already,' Bastian retorted.

6

Captain Brett Mallory had been expecting some kind of report from Bastian. But Bastian wasn't the type to make reports. So no wire had come and Mallory had to be content with pacing the floor occasionally and imagining scenarios in his head about what might be happening in Medicine Bend.

But then his impatient wait ended with Riley busting into his office waving a written message at him. It was from Ethan Purvis.

'Good news, Captain! He's already got two of them.'

Mallory, in his shirtsleeves, rose from his desk. 'Let me see that.'

He took the paper and read, and as he read, his face relaxed. He sat down again heavily, the paper still in his hand.

'By Jesus, I knew I sent the right man!'

'Bobo and that one called Daddy are dead.' Riley grinned. 'I knew he was good.' Riley had liked Bastian on first sight. 'But did you read the second part there?'

Mallory looked down again at the paper.

'Oh. He was shot.'

'Purvis says he'll be OK. But the rest of the gang was gone when Bastian arrived. They rode into the Territory. And Purvis says Bastian is going after them.'

'I see that,' Mallory said more soberly. 'Good.'

Riley took a seat beside Mallory's desk. 'The Territory is out of our jurisdiction, Captain.'

Mallory sighed. 'I know. But Bastian isn't a sworn-in Ranger, you know. He's a contract agent. He's under no obligation to observe rules of jurisdiction.' He put the paper down. 'And that's just the way I want it.'

'But wait, Captain. He is there under the authority of the Texas Rangers. Hell, he could get himself arrested by some federal marshal.'

'There isn't a marshal within five hundred miles of where he's going,' Mallory assured him.

'What about his wound? Should he be continuing with this right now? Wouldn't you feel a little responsible if that got him killed?'

Mallory looked at his young aide's innocent face. 'Yes, I might feel some guilt for a while. But if he puts Gabriel and all or most of his people six feet under, I'll be able to live with that.' He held Riley's questioning look with a firm, unwavering eye.

'What if they find out he's coming?'

'Who's going to tell them? Purvis?' Mallory sat back on his chair. Things were going pretty much as he had hoped. The Gabriel gang and all other outlaws in several states would find out what it was like to kill a Texas Ranger. Even if it wasn't a Ranger who taught them the lesson.

'Don't fret about it, Riley. I know Bastian a bit better than you. I kept the peace with him a long time ago. I know a prudent better would put his money on Gabriel. But I've seen him operate, and I would never bet against him. Just let it play out. I'm sure it will be all right.'

Riley nodded doubtfully. 'I wish I had your confidence, Captain. In my head, it's sixty-forty against our ever seeing him again.'

Mallory eyed him soberly. 'We'll see, Riley. We'll see.'

* * *

In Kiowa Junction Simon Gabriel and Cottonwood Eddie were at the Sumner Clinic. The gang had settled into a small boarding house run by a widower named Humphreys, and Gabriel had decided to stay on a few days before traveling on to Fort Repulse. Pedro Rueda was sitting in the parlor of the house with Humphreys, talking about stagecoach routes, and Thelma was out in back of the house shooting at targets. She could throw a silver dollar into the air and then hit it with her Harrington & Richardson .38 before the coin hit the ground. She considered herself another Annie Oakley, but had never really gotten that good.

At the clinic Gabriel was having his boil lanced. He was in the examination room with Sumner and Maggie Spencer, and Maggie actually did the lancing. Gabriel didn't usually get interested in women when he was involved in a project, but he had liked the looks of Maggie as soon as she walked into the room. She was the most beautiful woman he had seen in a year on the trail.

'Now, this is going to hurt some, Mr Gabriel. There's no other way to do it. Just hold real still.' She and the doctor knew who Gabriel was the minute he walked in. They had been warned about him by Ethan Purvis.

Dr Sumner was preparing an ointment to apply to the boil when Maggie was finished. He and Maggie exchanged a look behind Gabriel's back. Sumner would have used a scalpel on Gabriel if he thought he could get away with it.

Maggie inserted a needle into Gabriel's neck, and he grunted in pain.

'What are you using back there, an ice pick?' he asked with a harsh grin.

'It's draining very nicely,' Maggie reported to him. She had her hair down long on her shoulders, and her figure in the white medical coat was eye-catching. She swabbed the site of the boil, and joined the doctor at a medicine counter.

'Yeah. It feels better already,' Gabriel admitted. 'Say, you know what you're doing, girl!'

'Thanks,' she said abruptly. She was nervous with Gabriel there.

Dr Sumner came over and applied the ointment. He had hoped that if the gang stopped in town, he and Maggie would have no contact with any of them.

That will heal up in a few days, Mr Gabriel. You don't have to return here.'

Gabriel paid him no attention. He rose from the chair where they had seated him, and walked over to Maggie.

'I owe you big time, sweetheart. What's your name?'

She hesitated. 'Maggie.'

Gabriel grinned at her, looking her over carefully. She turned to face him and he saw the lovely green eyes.

'Maggie. I like that name. Mine is Simon, Maggie. It's a real pleasure to meet you.'

Maggie suddenly felt very uncomfortable. She was afraid of him, but didn't want him to know that.

'If you're the Simon Gabriel who robs banks, I can't say the feeling is mutual,' she said quietly.

Gabriel smiled a pleasant smile, and touched her cheek with his hand. She flinched, but didn't move away.

'It's a forgivable failing,' he said easily. 'I think you and me could be real good friends.'

'I don't think that's possible,' she replied, a bit breathlessly.

'Well. I'll be here a few days. Maybe I can change your mind,' Gabriel said in a half-whisper. At that point Dr Sumner hastily intervened.

'Didn't you say you wanted us to see

Edward Guthrie for facial burns? We're ready for him now, Mr Gabriel.'

Gabriel turned from Maggie with a last intimate grin.

'Oh, yeah. Eddie. Got some grease in the face. A damn cry-baby about it. But I thought you might have a salve or something.'

'I'm sure we can find something to make it more comfortable,' Sumner said. 'Can you get him in here for us?'

'Oh, sure.' Gabriel turned back to Maggie once more. 'I'll see you later, honey.'

Gabriel went out into a small waiting room, where Eddie was the only other patient waiting. Gabriel sent him in to see the doctor and sat himself down, thinking about Maggie. He decided he had to make time for this one. She was special. She could make big money in one of the big dance halls in Dallas, if she only knew it.

But then Rueda came in, about to change Gabriel's mood completely.

'Oh, good. You're still here,' he said.

He sat down beside Gabriel and lowered his voice. 'Sweet Daddy is dead.'

Gabriel slitted his dark eyes. 'What?'

'Daddy is dead. Some drifter just rode in from Medicine Bend. He told Humphreys and Humphreys told me.'

'Where's this drifter?'

'He rode out already. But he seemed sure about it. Daddy was killed in a gunfight.'

'A gunfight? Who could kill Daddy in a gunfight?'

'There was a man dressed in black. No badge.'

Gabriel's face settled into hard lines. 'There's a bounty hunter. They call him the Preacher.'

'Daddy didn't have a big bounty on him. Why would this Preacher bother?'

Gabriel rose from his seat red-faced. 'How the hell would I know? There are fifty reasons why men get into a drawdown!'

'We haven't heard from Bobo yet, either. *Dios mio*, this is a mystery!'

Gabriel got his anger under control,

and when he spoke again it was in a low, deliberate tone.

'It's no mystery. Some bank or stage line we hit has decided to up the ante on us. And this Preacher got his appetite whetted.'

'He maybe got Bobo too. Right, boss?'

Gabriel sighed heavily. Five minutes ago things had looked rosy. It was amazing how fast they could change.

'That's possible. And if those rewards are out on all of us, that swamp scum might be headed here.'

'Well, that would be good, wouldn't it? With four of us here to give him a big welcome? Instead of always looking behind our backs later?'

Gabriel settled his dark hat back on to his head. He turned and opened the door into the examination room, startling Maggie and the doctor. Maggie was just applying some ointment to Eddie's face.

'All right, that's enough of that. Come on, Eddie. We've got business to discuss. At the house.'

Eddie never argued with Gabriel. Especially when Gabriel was upset, as he was now. He rose from a chair without letting Maggie finish.

'Sure, Simon.'

'Take this ointment with you, in case you need it,' Maggie suggested calmly.

Eddie nodded, took the jar of ointment, and left with Gabriel and Rueda.

Maggie and the doctor stared after them for a long moment.

'What was that all about?' the doctor wondered.

'Something has happened,' Maggie said seriously. 'Gabriel acted like a different man.'

'Unfortunately, that different man is the real Gabriel,' the doctor commented. 'But I think this might be good for you. Gabriel was so distracted he didn't even glance at you when he came in here this time.'

'I wish I could count on that,' she replied. 'I didn't like the way he was looking at me before.'

'Maybe you should take a few days

off and get out of town,' Sumner suggested. 'I can't defend you against a gun-slinger, Maggie. And it would kill me if he hurt you.'

'I'm needed at the clinic,' she said, 'and that's where I'll be, whether they stay or leave. I have a gun at my house, and I know how to use it.'

Sumner sighed. 'I don't know if that would help, Maggie.'

'I'm just glad Jonah hasn't arrived yet,' she said. 'I wouldn't want him mixed up in something like this. He's just an innocent child.'

'Well, let's forget Gabriel. Bring me tomorrow's appointment list.'

She gave him a lovely smile. 'I'll be right back with it.'

*　*　*

At the rooming house, Gabriel was gathering his people to him. He had enlightened Eddie with the news from Medicine Bend, and Eddie walked to the house as if in a trance. Once there,

Gabriel sent Rueda out to fetch Thelma while he settled Eddie down in Gabriel's room. Rueda found Thelma just finishing up her shooting, which she did almost daily. She was ejecting shell casings from her revolver when Rueda found her.

'We got news from Medicine Bend. The boss wants to see you.'

Her heavy face was damp with perspiration. She stood as tall as Rueda, and that had always bothered him. She reloaded her gun, and frowned at him.

'What? News from our delinquent partners in crime? Hey, look, I've got one of these left.' She handed him a silver dollar. 'Throw it into the air. As high as you can loft it.'

'For God's sake, Thelma.'

'Come on. It will take a second.'

He took the coin and threw it high into the air, so far that he hoped Thelma couldn't see it. But in the next second she had fired off one quick shot, and he saw the coin spinning as it plummeted back to earth. She went and retrieved it and showed it to him with a big grin.

'Look at that! Do you know anybody who can do that, Pedro dear?' The coin had a hole through its center.

Rueda took it reluctantly. They all knew she was the best shot of the group. That irritated Rueda, too.

'Very nice, but you'll never be Annie Oakley,' he said with an easy grin.

'Who says?' she challenged belligerently, holstering the revolver. 'I'll go face to face with her any time, *hombre*. Bring her on!'

'Sweet Daddy is dead,' he said.

Thelma stared at him unblinking, unflinching. She looked down at the ground. When she looked up there were tears in her eyes.

'Are you sure?'

'*Madre mia!* I didn't know you could cry!'

She wiped at an eye. 'I'm not crying. Don't you dare tell Gabriel I was crying. You understand me?'

Rueda shrugged. 'I thought it was

sympatico. But I won't say anything.'

Thelma was herself again. 'Let's go inside.'

When they all were gathered in Gabriel's room, and Thelma knew everything they knew, including Gabriel's conjectures, Gabriel began discussing their future. He was sitting hatless on the edge of his cast-iron bed, a look on his face that they had never seen there before. It was a look of worry. Thelma sat beside him on the bed. Eddie occupied a big, soft chair, and Rueda leaned against a wall.

'So this is the situation. Bobo might be on his way here, or he might also be dead. We'll have to plan like he's gone. That leaves just four of us, and I wanted more than that to take that Territorial Bank at Fort Repulse. Every move I planned involved six people.'

'The James brothers started off with just two of them,' Eddie suggested. 'We can surely take it with four.'

Gabriel gave him a hard look. 'Would you take that damn ointment off? You look like a circus clown. It's distracting.'

Eddie looked sheepish. He took a kerchief and wiped some of the ointment off.

'She put it there,' he groused, gesturing toward Thelma.

'Don't forget it, either,' Thelma said bitterly. She felt hollow inside after the news about Daddy. They had paid special attentions to each other.

'This Preacher may be coming here,' Gabriel went on, ignoring the exchange between them. 'If he does, I want him taken out, once and for all.' He looked over at Thelma. 'This is probably your doing, you know.'

'What does that mean?' she demanded indignantly.

'You killed the Texas Ranger. Remember? I been thinking about it. I don't think we got bounties on us, *if* we have, because of any bank hold-up. I think the Rangers did this.'

'Maybe,' Thelma responded. 'But you seemed pretty happy at the time I pulled that trigger on him.'

Gabriel met her look. 'I'm not

placing blame here. I'm just pointing out the probable cause of some bounty hunter taking an interest in us.'

'If he comes here I'll put one through his black heart,' Thelma growled.

'Not if I see him first,' Rueda put in.

'Maybe he'll find us together,' Eddie opined. 'And we can all three take him down.' Eddie wasn't made for face-downs.

Gabriel nodded. 'I know how capable you all are. That's why I'm comfortable with my new plan.'

'New plan?' Eddie said. He didn't like changes in plans.

'I was going to stick around here a few days, then take all of you to Fort Repulse, where we would look that bank over. But that's out now. I'm riding there alone, and leaving you here for a few extra days to see if the Preacher shows. If he does, I want him dead, I don't care how you do it. Do I make myself clear?'

'Absolutely,' Thelma told him.

'If he doesn't show within a week,

he's not coming. Then you can all meet me at the Crossroads Hotel there and we'll finalize plans for taking that bank. Without thinking we have to be looking over our shoulders for some back-shooter all the time.' He had reluctantly given up on Maggie because of this news.

'It is a fine plan,' Rueda spoke up. 'And if this Preacher shows up here, he is already a walking dead man.'

Gabriel nodded. 'That's all I wanted to hear,' he said smoothly.

7

The weather had cooled off again, and had made riding easier for Jonah and Bastian as they headed for Kiowa Junction and Jonah's meeting with his aunt whom he had never known.

At the end of their first day of riding, Bastian encamped them not far from where the Gabriel gang had stopped almost a week before. As Jonah had promised, he was no trouble. He sweated in the midday sun, but did not complain. Bastian gave him the yellow neckerchief back to protect against perspiration, and stopped regularly underneath cottonwood trees to allow Jonah some relief from the saddle.

At their camp Jonah gathered firewood without being asked, and then helped Bastian heat up some beans and side pork. They sat on their saddles at the low fire, and there was no conversation until they were almost finished. Jonah looked up from his tin plate.

'Have you killed many men?'

Bastian gave him a narrow look. 'Eat your beans.'

'You don't talk much, do you?'

Bastian sighed. 'No.'

Jonah forked up some beans. 'I'll return the yellow bandanna. When we get there. It looked good on you.'

Bastian shook his head. 'It looks better on you, kid. I'll go back to the lariat tie and black jacket now. Maybe I'm more comfortable that way. It suits me. A man can't change what he is.' He had also gone back to the white shirt under his vest. Once again there was no color on him at all.

'You looked good with the bandanna.'

'Before we get to Kiowa Junction I want you to wash up in a stream. To look good for your aunt.'

'I'm clean enough now. I don't stink. Do I?'

Bastian put his plate down on the ground and looked over at Jonah.

'I can't smell you. But I probably stink myself.'

Jonah laughed at that, and Bastian found he liked the sound of the boy's laughter. He would never have believed it, but he had actually liked having Jonah along on this ride. The boy took his mind off what lay ahead in Kiowa Junction.

'How old is your aunt?' he asked Jonah, just to make conversation.

'Oh, I don't know her. But she must be real old. Like my dad. She's his sister.'

'She must be looking forward to meeting you,' Bastian told him. 'You should try to make a good first impression.'

'I'm not going to kiss her,' Jonah said, sticking his chin out.

Bastian smiled. He didn't like to admit it, but he was actually forming an affection for the boy. It went against his whole character, made him uneasy, and he fought it on some subconscious level.

'You'll get along just fine,' he said after a moment.

The fire cracked and popped and sparks flew into the black night around them. Jonah put his plate down too, and regarded his tall companion with ill-hidden admiration.

'Why do you do this?'

Bastian's liking for Jonah dropped down a level or two. He frowned slightly. 'I do it for the money, kid.'

'Why don't you join the Rangers?'

Bastian grunted. 'I make more in a few weeks than they do in a year. Anyway, they have rules to go by. I don't.'

'You mean, you can kill the outlaws you go up against?'

Bastian eyed him straight-faced. 'Yes. That's what it means. Now go clean our plates with sand.'

Jonah rose. 'I don't mind. That you kill them.'

'Fine. Now do what I told you.'

A coyote wailed in the distance as Jonah found a sandy spot and cleaned the plates by rubbing sand over their surfaces. There was no water available except in their canteens. A short while later Bastian put him to bed in a bedroll, and kicked the fire out. There was no point in announcing your presence to other travelers who might or might not be friendly.

Jonah lay there looking up at a black, starry sky and wondering if he had it in him to be a bounty hunter. He would have to get himself a gun one of these days soon, and practice with it.

At last, after Bastian had lain down on his own bedroll, he said, 'Goodnight, Luther.'

Bastian looked over at the dark form across the guttering fire, and noted how small it was. Very small, in a big, sometimes dangerous world. He sighed lightly.

'Goodnight, Jonah.'

★ ★ ★

At the Sumner Clinic the next morning, Maggie Spencer was busy treating locals for various minor ailments, assisting Dr

Sumner in placing a cast on a broken ankle, applying medicinal cream to a blotched skin, and helping with various other minor problems as they presented themselves. But Maggie had the Gabriel gang on her mind.

She and the doctor knew that Gabriel himself had left town, and that gave her temporary relief. She had been afraid of his attentions to her. But there were three of them still there, Maggie had no idea why, and those who remained were a continuing threat to the town and the clinic.

During a noon break from work, after eating a light lunch at the clinic, Maggie walked down to the general store, which was just down the street from the rooming house where the three outlaws were staying. She figured the chance of running into one of them was nil. But she was wrong.

She was in the store, asking the price of tinned pears, when Pedro Rueda walked in. He spotted her immediately, and knew who she was. He walked over to the counter and leaned on it beside her. When she turned and saw him, a small gasp issued from her throat.

'Well!' Rueda grinned. 'The surprises we can get at the store, heh?'

She looked down and then turned back to the clerk, who looked nervous now.

'I'll take two cans of the pears,' she said. 'And that roll of ribbon we talked about.'

'Yes, ma'am,' the young clerk responded, giving Rueda a look before he went for the ribbon to wrap it.

'You are the one from the clinic, yes?' Rueda pressed her.

Maggie nodded. 'Yes. From the clinic.'

'I understand now what Gabriel was talking about.' He grinned.

Maggie found her courage. 'Would you please excuse me? I'm trying to conduct business here?'

'Oh, *sí*. Business. But life is not all business, is it, *señorita?* Bastian was going to pay you a visit to give you relaxation. All work and no play, right? I think he would not mind if I took his place in his absence.'

'Please leave me alone!' Maggie told him. The clerk was back with the ribbon and was putting it in a bag with the tinned pears.

'Don't bother the customers, sir,' the clerk said warily. 'I'll be with you in a moment.'

Rueda gave him a hard look. 'Do you want something, little man?'

'No, sir. I just don't want any trouble in here.'

Rueda turned from him to Maggie again. 'Listen. Where do you live, señorita? I will bring you a bottle of excellent mezcal tonight. We can have a good time. You understand?'

She turned hostilely on him. 'Keep away from me, you damned coward! I'll shoot you if you come near me.'

That outburst gave Rueda pleasure, and he laughed under his breath.

'A little firebrand, heh? I like it. It will make things much more interesting.'

Maggie took her bag of purchases

and left the store flushed in the face, with Rueda grinning after her.

All that afternoon Maggie was upset by her second encounter with the Gabriel gang. During the treatment of a half-dozen patients before closing time, she envisioned actually leaving town for a while, as Sumner had suggested. But her nephew Jonah could be delivered to her at any time, and she didn't want to be off somewhere else when he arrived. Especially with men like these in town.

About a half-hour after the clinic doors closed for the day, and while she was still there alone, cleaning up after the last patient, her judgement was vindicated.

Luther Bastian rode into town with Jonah.

Luther was glad to be there. The second day of riding had been hard on his wounded side, and the area was giving him some pain.

It didn't take him long to find the clinic. Maggie had just stepped back into the waiting room in preparation for leaving when Bastian walked in from outside.

She stopped where she stood, and stared at him. He was more frightening in his appearance than Gabriel had been, or Rueda. The tall, dark figure emanated danger in his black suit and hat and the deadly-looking revolver on his belt, which caught the viewer's eye first.

She caught her breath and held it. 'Who are you?'

He removed his hat, and made a face because of the pain.

'Luther Bastian, ma'am. Are you Maggie Spencer?'

Just then Jonah appeared tentatively from behind Bastian. 'You're Aunt Maggie, aren't you!'

Maggie's face brightened, and a wide smile came on to it.

'Jonah! Is it really you?'

She moved quickly over to the boy, bent down and hugged him tightly. Jonah gave Bastian a look past her head.

'I can't believe you're here!' she exclaimed. 'And you're so big! You were a baby the last time I saw you. You're very handsome, you know.'

'I don't kiss,' Jonah said quickly.

'Of course you don't,' she said, rubbing a hand through his tousled hair. 'I'm so glad you got here safely. Did this gentleman bring you?'

Jonah nodded. 'This is my friend,' he said proudly.

Maggie turned to Bastian. 'I'm sorry, you startled me. I guess I expected someone — different would bring him.'

Bastian was busy taking in her youth and her beauty.

'I'm surprised, too. I thought you'd be older.'

'I was a lot younger than my brother.' She smiled uncertainly at him. Now that he had spoken so gently to her, and she got a closer look at his face, she admitted to herself that she liked his looks. The strong face, the dark eyes. His very masculine look. He gave off an aura of easy confidence that filled the room with its intensity. She blushed slightly under his gaze.

'Jonah was no trouble at all,' he went on. 'I think you two will get along just fine.'

'I think so, too.' She smiled, hugging Jonah to her. Jonah decided he liked being hugged.

Bastian moved again, and grimaced. Maggie saw the look, and frowned prettily. 'Are you all right?'

'Oh, I'll be fine. I'm just trying to heal this place on my side.'

'Well, this is a clinic, you know. Let me take a look at it.'

'That won't be necessary, ma'am.'

'I'll say what's necessary here in the clinic,' she insisted. 'Here. Let's get that jacket off.'

Bastian had already rearmed himself fully, and when she removed the coat she saw the second gun, the Meriden revolver in the home-made shoulder holster. To Maggie, he was fairly bristling with guns.

'Goodness. Let's get that gun off you. That could be causing you pain.'

But when she got the harness off and

then undid his vest, she saw the blood on his white shirt.

'Oh! You're bleeding through a bandage!'

'That's temporary,' he assured her. 'It's the rib that's causing me trouble.'

'You come in the other room with me. I'll re-dress that wound.'

'It's a gunshot wound,' Jonah said with a big smile.

Maggie looked over at him soberly. 'I know, Jonah. Maybe you should wait out here.'

Jonah was tired. 'OK, Aunt Maggie.'

Maggie loved hearing that from him. She smiled. 'We'll be right back out.'

Inside the examination room, she took Bastian's vest and shirt off and was surprised at the athletic, muscular look of him. She found she liked it, along with the long, dark hair and dark eyes. Unlike the doctor, he didn't look like a man who would be intimidated by Simon Gabriel.

She put a new, smaller bandage on Bastian's wound, and retaped the rib. As he put the shirt back on she watched him with interest.

'You've been shot before, haven't you?'

He looked into her deep green eyes. 'You must attract a lot of men to the clinic for very minor ailments.'

She blushed again. 'Thanks, Mr Bastian.'

'Call me Luther,' he told her.

'All right. Luther. Why do you wear so many guns?'

He sighed. 'Sometimes they're necessary. I go after wanted men for the rewards on them, Maggie.' He watched her face.

'I see.'

'Sorry if that bothers you. But it's how I make a living. I've gotten fairly good at it.'

'It doesn't bother me, Luther.'

His shirt was on again. 'I wanted to ask you. Have you seen any strangers in town in the past week?'

Her eyes clouded over. 'As a matter of fact, yes. That Simon Gabriel and his men are here. They've been to the clinic. But Gabriel rode out, and left the others here. Two men and a woman. The Mexican gave me some trouble at the store today. He's probably harmless.'

'None of them is harmless,' Bastian said evenly. 'Keep away from them.'

'Are you . . . after them?'

But Jonah had come into the room, unseen. 'He's already killed two of them,' he said with a big grin.

They both looked at him. 'Take it easy, kid,' Bastian said easily.

Maggie looked over at Bastian, sober-faced, and said nothing.

'Sorry,' Jonah said, seeing her face.

'Are you sure Gabriel is gone?' Bastian asked her.

'That's what I heard,' she replied quietly.

'Well, that's good and bad,' Bastian said to himself. He went back out into the waiting area and put the vest back on, and the shoulder harness. Then he carefully replaced the black jacket and the black Stetson. Once again he looked like the formidable figure who had walked in a short time ago.

'I hope that shoulder gun doesn't bother your side,' she offered.

'It will be all right, ma'am,' he told her. He turned to Jonah, and it struck him forcibly that their time together might be finished. 'Jonah. You've come into a good thing here. Make the most of it, you hear me?'

'I will, Luther,' Jonah said. 'But you're coming home with us, aren't you?'

They were both embarrassed. 'That's not possible, kid,' Bastian explained to him. 'Your aunt is a maiden lady. Oh, well. You'll figure it out.'

'Where will you be staying?' Maggie asked tentatively. 'The gang is at the only boarding house in town. They would know immediately if you checked in there.'

Bastian nodded. 'I can take that chance. Or maybe the doctor wouldn't mind if I slept here for the night. Push two chairs together.'

'Well, I'm sure he wouldn't mind,' Maggie said uncertainly.

'Take him home with us!' Jonah persisted. 'We've been on the trail for two days.'

'Jonah, for God's sake!'

'No, wait. There's a spare room with cots at my rented house. You can sleep there with Jonah. I'm moving a bed in for him later. Anyway, you won't be any trouble at all, Luther. I'll make you both a nice breakfast tomorrow morning. Then we'll figure it out as we go along.'

'Are you sure?' Bastian said. 'What will your neighbors say?'

She smiled a smile that he felt deep inside him. 'If they're more interested in me than these gunmen in town, so be it. I'm not concerned.'

'All right.' He studied her face for a moment. 'I don't want to get too personal. But a girl that looks like you. Unmarried? I don't get it.'

For the third time she crimsoned slightly. 'I had my chances. Things didn't quite work out. And recently I've been too busy at the clinic to think of things like that.'

'I shouldn't have asked. I've never been good with women.'

'Is that why you're still alone?'

He laughed lightly. 'A point well made. But I think the life I took up has more to do with it. Gunslingers don't get serious about women, Maggie. Their futures are too uncertain.'

Her pretty face went sober. 'I'm sorry about that.'

Jonah had been listening silently. 'You're not a regular gunslinger. You're like a Texas Ranger. Some of them are married.'

Bastian smiled at him. 'You go on home with Maggie. I'll get our mounts bedded at those stables we saw near here, then I'll walk on down to the house.'

'It's on this street, and has green shutters at the windows,' she told him. 'I'll set a lamp at the front door.'

They separated outside, and Maggie took Jonah home. She had been anticipating this moment with excitement ever since Ethan Purvis's wire to her about the grandfather's death. She had thought of Jonah from time to time, but it hadn't occurred to her on a serious level that she would ever gain custody of him. She had been without family for so long that she had never hoped for any kind of reunion, let alone this intimate taking-charge of a young nephew. The prospect of having Jonah with her now and for the future was a situation that made her burst with new happiness.

Jonah liked the house. It was bigger than the cabin he had shared with his grandfather, and had a brighter appearance. There were curtains on windows, and pleasant odors.

'Gramps would have liked this,' he said when they were seated on a small sofa in the neat, ordered parlor.

Maggie smoothed his hair. She liked his freckles. She liked his blue eyes. She liked the young masculinity of him. She would treat him like a son.

'I'm sorry for your loss, Jonah,' she said softly. 'You're a brave boy. To go through that, and then come all the way here.'

'I didn't like Medicine Bend any more,' Jonah said. 'They spoiled it for me. The Gabriel gang. They killed a Texas Ranger.'

'So they were there before coming here?'

He nodded. 'They hoorawed our mayor. I tried to kill one of them. I'm not very good with a gun.'

'Oh, dear! I didn't know,' Maggie said, her eyes becoming moist. 'You poor boy!'

'I'm all right,' Jonah told her. 'I was all right from the minute Luther rode in. The Rangers sent him, you know.'

'No. I didn't.'

'I like him, Aunt Maggie.' He looked up at her. 'I like him a lot.'

She hesitated, then nodded. 'I can understand that. But he'll be gone soon, Jonah.'

'I wish he would stay right here,' Jonah said pensively. 'You know. With us.'

Maggie didn't know what to say. 'I'm sure a man like that has his plans, Jonah. Remember, he just met us.' She rose. 'Come on, let's go make up your cots so they'll be ready when he gets here.'

'OK.'

'And you can call me just Maggie, Jonah. That will be fine.'

'Thanks. That's swell.'

★   ★   ★

Down at the stables Bastian was delivering the black stallion and Jonah's dun mare to the liveryman. The fellow had been ready to go home for the night, and acted impatient about receiving the animals.

'Sure, I'll board them. I got three others in here, but I got room. Let's just get on with it. I got a jug of whiskey at home with my name on it.'

They unsaddled the animals and got them installed as Bastian removed the three guns from his mount's irons: the Winchester 1866 lever-action rifle, the Remington 8-gauge double-barreled shotgun, and the Webley-Pryse 14.6-millimeter pistol, from his saddle-bag. The gun and the rifle needed oiling, and he figured on doing that before he slept that night.

Bastian leaned the long guns against the wall near the big double doors, and turned to the liveryman. 'I'll take these with me.'

'That's a lot of hardware, mister. Are you with them boys up at the boarding house?'

Bastian made a sour face. 'Look. I want these mounts fed and watered before you leave. They had a hard day on the trail.'

The liveryman, a husky fellow with a three-days beard, chuckled.

'You got here too late for that, mister. I'm on my way home. If you want, you can stay and hay them down. There's a trough of water out back there.'

Bastian was exasperated. He pushed his coat back and showed the Peacemaker boldly in the dim light of dusk. He walked over to the liveryman. The fellow backed up and hit the wall behind him, wide-eyed.

'Do you want trouble with me, pot-belly?'

'Uh. No, I don't. I was just saying . . . '

'I'll be paying you top dollar to tend these animals,' Bastian told him. 'I don't care if you don't get home till breakfast. I want them tended to now. Is that quite clear?'

The liveryman licked dry lips. 'Yeah. Sure, take it easy.'

'And if that stallion doesn't look even better when I return, you know who's going to wish he'd done a better job?'

'Me.'

'That's right. Now. Those other three mounts. Do they belong to the men over at the boarding house?'

'Yes, sir.'

'I'll sell those animals and their gear to you for the cost of boarding this stallion and mare.'

'But you don't own them horses.'

'If I can deliver them to you is it a deal?'

The liveryman nodded quickly. 'Sure. They're worth three times what I'd charge you.'

Bastian picked up the shotgun and rifle: 'Good. I'll be back.'

'Say, mister. Who are you?'

Bastian gave him a final look. 'Somebody you don't want to know.'

It was just a short walk back to Maggie's house in the growing darkness. Bastian was relaxed as he walked, having no idea that, while he was in the hostelry, Pedro Rueda had left the rooming-house, walking right past the stables, and headed down to Maggie's place.

He was looking forward to a long evening's entertainment.

8

Rueda had been thinking about Maggie ever since their meeting at the general store. The dark hair. The green eyes. The way she filled out her clothing. It was enough to make a man's blood boil, if he let himself imagine what all that could mean to him.

There weren't many women like Maggie on the frontier. The saloon girls were over-used, over-gussied-up ladies of the evening who had lost their innocence and their magic long ago. Almost all women of Maggie's calibre had married and gone off to the big city somewhere. You never found one in a remote medical clinic in a one-horse town. If you did, you were a fool not to do something about it.

So Rueda had left the rooming-house after an evening meal with Eddie and Thelma and, without telling them, he bought a bottle of *mezcal* at the small, dirty local saloon and walked down to Maggie's house with it. He had enquired where she lived, at the store after she left.

It was about the time that Bastian was giving his last-minute instructions to the stable-owner when Rueda arrived at Maggie's house and knocked at her front door.

Maggie thought it would be Bastian when she opened her door, and her face showed surprise and mild shock when she saw Rueda. She gasped, but did not speak.

'*Buenas noches*, Señorita Maggie.' Rueda grinned broadly. 'I hope this is not a bad time? Look, I come bearing a gift.' He held the bottle of *mezcal* up so she could see it. 'This will start an evening off right, *sí*?'

Maggie frowned at him now. 'I told you at the store. Just leave me alone. Please.'

She started to close the door again, but he stopped her.

'I don't think you understand. This evening together is going to happen, *hijita*.' He pushed past her and entered her parlor, closing the door behind him.

'How dare you! Get out of my house, damn you.'

He grabbed her arm and held it in a vicelike grip. His heavy features were now more businesslike.

'Now, now. You will quiet down after a few swallows from this fine bottle. I got it special, you know, just for you.'

Jonah's voice came from the adjacent room. 'I like this cot! You will, too!' Thinking the male voice he heard was that of Bastian.

'Go to bed, Jonah!' Maggie called back tensely.

'Who?' Rueda frowned.

Then Jonah appeared in the doorway. A smile on his young face evaporated quickly when he saw Rueda.

'You!' he said loudly.

'Jesus y Maria!' Rueda exclaimed under his breath. 'The loco boy that tried to kill me.'

'If I had a gun you'd be dead now!' Jonah said fiercely. He went over to Maggie. 'Let go of her! Get out of here!'

Rueda did release Maggie. Then he

backhanded Jonah, slapping him hard across the face and sending him backward to the sofa, where Jonah fell on to it with his nose bleeding.

Maggie screamed out briefly, then began hitting out at Rueda.

'You damn animal! Leave him alone! Get out of my house!'

Rueda grabbed her arm again. 'How did he get here? Who brought him?'

'Let go of me,' she shouted at him. She tried to break free, her blouse tore away slightly at her bosom and Rueda was momentarily distracted from Jonah.

'I'll find it all out later, anyway,' he said, looking her over hungrily. 'For now, I'll lock this little coyote in the other room. While we have a good old Mexican fiesta, sí?'

He threw the bottle on to a nearby chair and pulled her close to him, in preparation for kissing her. But then she let out a very loud scream, right into his swarthy face.

Outside, Luther Bastian had just arrived at the house, carrying his two long guns.

He had been too far away to hear Maggie's first scream, but this second one came to him loud and clear. He had just been going to knock on the door to announce his presence when he heard it.

A heavy frown contorted his face as he set the rifle up against the house and took the shotgun in both hands. He guessed immediately that it must be one or more of the Gabriel gang inside. If it were more than one, the shotgun would be a better weapon than the Colt Peacemaker. Another scream issued from the house; he backed up a step, then kicked out at the door.

The door slammed inward, making both Maggie and Rueda jump. Jonah was still in mild shock on the sofa, blood on his lower face. Seeing him, anger rose in Bastian's chest. Rueda had been holding Maggie close to him, his back to the door, but had turned at the sound of the door crashing inward, and now stared hard at Bastian.

'So.'

'That's right,' Bastian growled.

In that moment of distraction Maggie broke free from Rueda and fell on the sofa beside Jonah, cradling him in her arms. She was crying.

'You brought the *niño*,' Rueda said, regaining his composure.

'What the hell do you think you're up to here?' rasped Bastian in a low, menacing tone. The shotgun was leveled at Rueda's groin. Behind him a chunk of splintered wood fell heavily to the floor.

'I made a little visit to the nurse. I have this wart on my arm,' Rueda replied with a hard grin.

Bastian felt frustration building in him. He didn't want this here. Not in front of Jonah and Maggie. They were already traumatized by events.

'You and your friends. You were waiting for me, weren't you?'

'Gabriel wanted it over with, since you seem so persistent, Señor Preacher.' Rueda showed no fear of Bastian. He was almost as good as Thelma in accuracy, and as fast as Gabriel.

'Kill him, Luther!' Jonah cried out.

But the boy had no idea what a shotgun would do to a man. Or how Bastian's death might affect him. Rueda saw the hesitation and grew confident.

'Maybe you lost your touch, Preacher? A scattergun over the Peacemaker?' Bastian's coat was open, and Rueda spotted a small stain on Bastian's dark vest. 'Ah, I think I see. Bobo put one in you, didn't he? Or was it Daddy? You don't trust yourself with the sidearm now.'

'Maybe you'll get a chance to find out,' Bastian said. 'But not here.'

'Who says not here?' Rueda countered, enjoying this now. 'If one of us must go, it will have to be you, I think. I must still have my wart looked at.' His grin was crooked now.

'Don't press your luck, Mex. It's you that's leaving. I sleep here.'

'*Caramba*! So you beat me to her, heh?' Rueda was very relaxed. Then his face changed again. 'Your finger isn't even on the trigger of that big gun. I can put two in you before you can unload that old thing.'

'Are you sure you want to see if it works out that way?' Bastian asked him in a low, even voice.

Rueda hesitated, then took a deep breath. 'Oh, well. This works just as well. Everybody will know the Preacher backed down from a draw with Pedro Rueda. Yes, I like it!' He walked over to Bastian. 'I suggest you get out of town fast, señor. Or you will never leave.'

'Goodnight, Rueda,' Bastian told him.

Rueda laughed in his throat and left the house, closing the busted door after him to protect his back.

Bastian laid the shotgun down and went over to the sofa. He looked Jonah over and took a handkerchief from Maggie to wipe the blood from his face.

'You'll be just fine,' Bastian told him.

'Thank God you came,' Maggie said.

'You should have killed him,' Jonah offered.

Bastian smiled. 'It's time for bed, kid.'

Maggie was still shaky inside. 'I'll wash him up. Tomorrow maybe I can find you a clean shirt. Are you coming to bed?'

'Maybe a little later,' Bastian said. He retrieved the Remington 8-gauge and took it back to the sofa with him. 'I don't trust that Mexican to let it go tonight. I'll join the boy soon.'

'Well. We're going to bed. Please be careful, Luther.' She caught his gaze and held it, and he liked the look in her green eyes.

'I will. Goodnight.' He realized he hadn't said goodnight to a woman since his adolescent years. Well, maybe a saloon girl now and then. But they didn't count.

The house grew silent in the next half-hour, and Bastian fought sleep. He was sitting back on the sofa, in his vest. He had removed the shoulder holster, but the Colt still hung on his belly, like a cobra waiting to strike. The shotgun was propped on the sofa beside him.

Almost an hour after Maggie and Jonah were bedded down he heard the slight noise outside. Most men wouldn't have caught the metallic click, so soft, just outside the open window at the front of the parlor. Bastian knew it was lucky that he had, in his weary condition.

He didn't move on the sofa. Carefully, he slid his finger into the trigger assembly of the shotgun, without visibly moving the gun itself. He tried to look asleep, using patience he had learned over the years.

Then it happened. A form appeared in the window and grew larger. It was Rueda's face and torso, showing plainly now in the window. Rueda was looking right at him, and had assessed that he was asleep, Bastian's eyes being hooded.

You damn skunk, Bastian thought, focusing on the face in the window.

Then Rueda's arm came up slowly and silently, and his hand held the wicked-looking Remington .44 that he always carried at his side. He aimed the gun at Bastian's chest.

In that second, though, Bastian raised the muzzle of his own Remington and squeezed one of its two triggers.

The booming blast rent the air like a cannon, and the shot hit Rueda full-on in his face and chest. The buckshot blew Rueda's face away, almost decapitating him, and sent him careening off his feet into the blackness. His gun fired into the side of the house as he went down, and then silence settled in.

The buckshot had also shredded the windowpane and glass above the open part, and left holes in the wall around the window.

There was a scream from Maggie's bedroom. By the time Bastian had got on to his feet, she was in her doorway.

'My God! What is it?'

'He came back,' Bastian said easily. 'Sorry, Maggie.'

Now Jonah appeared in the doorway of the other bedroom.

'What happened?'

'I have to check outside. You two stay put. You don't want to see this.'

Maggie went and hugged Jonah to her.

'Oh, God! Oh, God!'

'He killed him, didn't he?' Jonah said in a hushed tone. 'He killed Rueda.'

Bastian walked outside and found

Rueda on his back in the darkness.

Except for the Mexican hat lying near by, and the Spanish vest and trousers, nobody would have been able to identify him. His head had been destroyed by the blast.

Bastian stood over him for a long moment.

'You had to try, didn't you? So you got all the credit.'

But Rueda was in no condition to reply. Like Bobo, he had miscalculated.

Bastian went back inside, and laid the shotgun down.

'Is he dead?' Maggie asked in a half-whisper.

Bastian nodded.

'Good,' Jonah said, beside her. Eyes big.

'Don't you go out there,' Bastian told him.

Maggie suddenly began sobbing, releasing her hold on Jonah and leaning against the wall. Bastian went over to her and touched her shoulder. She surprised him by turning and putting her head on his chest.

He liked the feel of her against him. Something reached deep inside him that he had never felt before. It made him feel a little breathless.

'It's all right now,' he told her. 'He's the one you had to worry about.'

'This is all too . . . terrible for me,' she admitted, wiping at an eye. 'I'm sorry. I don't mean it that way.'

'I know what you mean,' he said.

Jonah was smiling at them. Hoping. After a moment, he said, 'Can I look out the window?'

'No.' As Maggie released her hold on him Bastian held her face in his hand.

'You're a very strong girl, Maggie. I like that.'

She looked into his dark eyes. 'I'm so glad it was you who brought Jonah.'

'I am, too. Now, do you have a shovel somewhere around here? I want to get him under ground. Before dawn.'

'Shouldn't we be taking him to the mortician?' she wondered.

'Then the others would know what happened,' Jonah told her.

They both looked at him. 'You're learning too fast, kid.' Bastian smiled at him.

Jonah held his gaze. 'I'm glad I know you, Luther.'

Bastian just stood there for a moment. 'I'm glad, too, Jonah.'

'We're friends, aren't we?'

Maggie looked over at Bastian to see his reaction.

'Yes, I guess we are, kid. Now let Maggie put you back to bed while I get this job done.'

Jonah agreed to that, knowing he couldn't sleep. But he wanted to please Bastian.

Bastian dragged Rueda's body out into a thicket behind the house, dug a shallow grave and put Rueda in it. When he got back to the house Maggie was waiting for him on the sofa with a cup of coffee.

They sat silently together while Bastian drank part of the coffee, then set it aside. After a while he said: 'I'll be out of here early tomorrow, Maggie.

193

And I won't be back till it's over.'

'You have to go after the others now?'

'I have a contract,' he said. 'I always honor my agreements. Especially with friends.'

'Maybe I shouldn't say this. But I can't think about it. That you might not . . . you know.'

Bastian turned to study her lovely face. 'I like that, Maggie.'

'I've just met you. But it seems like I've known you for ever. I'm sorry. I usually don't talk like this to men.'

'I know that.'

They sat there locking at the broken window and door. Maggie was clutching a night-robe around her. Bastian moved his left arm and made a face. The rib was still healing. She looked over at him.

'You don't seem like a man who would do this for a living.'

He hesitated. 'Something happened to one of my family, Maggie. It turned my world upside down. Made me see everything through a dark lens.'

'What the world can take away, the world can give back,' she said softly.

He returned her look. 'I'd like to think that. I really would.' Another long pause.

'Will they come after you? Or wait for you to make the first move?'

'They don't even know I'm here yet. That might give me an element of surprise. Once they know they'll probably press a confrontation. Or maybe try an ambush. Gabriel wants me dead.'

Her eyes teared up, but he didn't see it.

'Where will you be?' she asked.

'I'll sleep at the stables with my horse if it comes to that. I'll be gone from your place by dawn. I'm paying for the repairs up front there.'

'The repairs are the least of my worries,' she said disconsolately.

He sighed. 'Maggie. These are very dangerous people. They murdered a Texas Ranger like it was nothing. That has to be answered. And at the moment, there's nobody but me to do the job. Go to bed and forget about it.'

'I'll make you breakfast before you leave.'

He nodded. 'All right.'

'And Jonah will want to see you.'

'Fine. Go to bed. I'm going to stay right here on the sofa.'

'I'll see you at dawn.'

★   ★   ★

Several hours later, Cottonwood Eddie got out of bed tiredly at the Humphreys boarding house. He and Rueda had shared a room with two beds, and the first thing Eddie did upon rising was look over to the second bed to see if Rueda was up. When he saw the bed he stopped and stared hard. It was still made up from the night before.

'What the devil?' he muttered under his breath.

He dressed hastily, hurried down the hall to Thelma's room and went in without knocking. Thelma had just dressed and was strapping on her gunbelt when he arrived. She turned from a wall mirror to greet him with a frown.

'Hey. Don't you ever knock?'

She dressed like her exemplar Annie Oakley, with a heavy skirt and knee-boots. Her thick hair was pulled back severely in a bun, and her thick features looked more masculine than feminine.

'Rueda isn't here. His bed hasn't been slept in.'

Her frown deepened. 'Are you sure? Maybe he was up early and made his bed up.'

'That greaser never made a bed in his life,' Eddie said acidly.

'So what are you saying?'

'I'm saying, he went over to that nurse's house last night. He told me so. He had a thing for her. He's almost as bad as Bobo. Anyway, it looks like he never came back from there.'

She laughed harshly. 'He's probably still in bed with the nurse. Unlike some people I know, he knows how to satisfy his urges.'

'He's never stayed overnight with any

woman,' Eddie persisted. 'I'm telling you, something is wrong. I got a bad feeling about this.'

'You've got a bad feeling about most things. Let's go downstairs and get some breakfast. I could eat my horse.'

'Oh, Jesus!'

'What?'

'The Preacher might be here already. Rueda might be laying deader than thunder on some deserted side street.'

Thelma thought that over for a moment. 'Hmm. It's possible. Look. Walk on down to the livery stables and see if there's new mounts billeted there. The word is, the Preacher rides a black stallion. I'm going on down for breakfast.'

'Well, OK. That's a good idea. Stay put here till I get back.'

'I'll save you a barley cake.'

A few minutes later Eddie was on his way to the stables at the same time as Bastian was stopping in at the local saloon to see if either of his opponents had arrived there yet.

Eddie arrived at the stables just as the owner, the same fellow Bastian had spoken to earlier, was throwing a pail of comb-curry water out on to the ground. He looked up at Eddie and recognized him immediately.

'Oh, Mr Brown. I just fed your animal. Will you be taking him out?'

Eddie stood an inch taller than the other man, and scowled down on him now.

'No, no. Listen. Has anybody else boarded a horse with you since we did? In the last day or two.'

'Why, yes. A tall, dark man came in here. Left two horses in my care. A stallion and a mare. They're back there in those back stalls.'

Eddie brushed past him and went down the aisle of stalls. When he came to the black stallion he just stopped and stared.

'Oh, Jesus!'

'Is something wrong, mister? Do you know the owner of that horse?'

'Was this man dressed all in black?'

Eddie said. 'Was he wearing a gun right here like this, on his belly?'

'Why, now that you mention it . . . '

Eddie had never considered himself much of a gun-fighter. He would much rather shoot unarmed innocents than shoot it out with somebody good with a gun. He felt his mouth go dry.

'He's here,' he said. 'And he's already killed Rueda.'

'Huh?'

Eddie leaned on the wall of the next stall. 'Now there's just two of us.'

The stable-owner watched his face curiously. 'Oh, I almost forgot. He sold me your three horses.'

Eddie turned to him blankly. 'He did what?'

'He seemed to think you wouldn't be needing them. Of course, if you still want them . . . '

Eddie turned to him fiercely. 'Shut up, damn you! Just shut up.'

Then he was hurrying out of the stables, heading back to the boarding house. Thoughts were tumbling through his head like blown weeds. The Preacher had never failed to collect on his man. The Preacher always came to kill. When you saw the Preacher come for you, you'd better find a way to kill him before he killed you. He could not be reasoned with. He could not be persuaded, or bought off. He was the angel of death.

By the time Eddie arrived back at the house Thelma had finished her breakfast and returned to her room. For the second time that morning he busted into her room without announcing his arrival. His face flushed.

Thelma was sitting on her bed, cleaning her very accurate Harrington & Richardson .38.

'My God, Eddie! How many times do I have to tell you?'

'He's here,' he said breathlessly.

She laid the gun down on the bed. 'You saw his mount?'

He nodded. 'He sold our horses to the owner of the stables.'

'Sold them? Have you been drinking, you numb-brain?'

I'm telling you. In his head, we're already dead.'

Thelma narrowed her eyes on him. 'Are you going to pieces on me, Eddie? What's the matter with you?'

Eddie had never liked Thelma. But since she burned his face, he had nursed a definite dislike of her.

'Nothing's the matter with me, woman! There's something the matter with you if this doesn't scare you.'

'Scare me? Me scared of that two-bit bounty hunter? He makes his money by ambushing men with their guards down. He probably shot Rueda in the back.'

'I think that stuff is all bull-pucky. The man is a Webster with guns, I heard Gabriel say so. It's clear as cloud peaks under sheet lightning. We got to ride out of here while we still have time.'

'Good God! Do you think I'm running from some yellow-belly killer for money? Do you really know how good I am, dimwit?' She picked the revolver up again. 'With this little fellow I can cut the buttons off his damn coat. I can fire the cartridges off his gunbelt. I can smash every knuckle in his gunhand before he can clear leather.'

Eddie lowered his voice. 'This isn't like target practice, Thelma. This is life or death. Our lives and our deaths. I'm not willing to take that gamble.'

'What do you mean?' She rose menacingly from the bed.

'I mean I'm riding out. To join Gabriel at Fort Repulse. I can rob a bank there. I've got no business here.'

'You've got the business of the Preacher,' she told him angrily, her gun in her hand. 'Gabriel told us to end it with him before we joined him. You ride there like this, he'll send you back here.'

'We'll see,' Eddie said. 'I'm riding.'

But Thelma came over to him and stuck the small revolver in his face.

'Now you listen to me. Your place is here with me, you little weasel. You're not going anywhere. You're not leaving my sight. And I'll blow your brains out if you try to run.'

Eddie was angry and scared at the same time. He had always been a little afraid of Thelma.

'Hey. Take it easy, I was just talking.'

'You stick right here and this will all be over today or tomorrow. I'll take the lead, you just back me up.'

'Hell. All right, Thelma. Maybe you know best.'

'I usually do,' she said with a hard grin.

9

In Fort Repulse Simon Gabriel stood at a teller's window at the Territorial Bank. He was clean-shaven, wearing a white shirt and tie under a dark vest, and was trying to look like a businessman despite the obvious scar across his square face.

'Yes, ma'am, that's right. I have a rather large amount of money to deposit with your fine bank.'

'Why, that's very nice.' The young, thin woman smiled at him. 'How much did you intend to deposit, sir?'

'Well, I'd prefer to discuss that with one of your officers. Is somebody available?'

'Of course. I'll take you over to our Mr Matthews if you'll step through that gate over there.'

A moment later Gabriel was standing before the desk of a prim-looking, bespectacled junior officer of the bank, who wore sleeve garters and a green visor. Gabriel repeated what he had told the teller.

'Well, we're glad you chose the Territorial, Mr Jones.' He rose with a wider smile than that of the teller, and shook Gabriel's hand. 'We have one of the finest institutions in the Territory, if I may brag a little. Your money will be very safe with us, I assure you.'

'Well, that's just what I wanted to ask about,' Gabriel said. 'Security. I don't want to sit home worrying about this very large sum of money I'm about to leave in your custody.' He was not wearing his Colt Army revolver, or any gun at all.

'Well, Mr Jones. What can I say to assure you?'

'Why don't you tell me about your vault? Guards? Things like that.'

In the next ten minutes, the officer took Gabriel into the big vault at the rear of the bank, explained the locking mechanism, and summarized how many guards were on duty at what hours. When they were back at the officer's desk Gabriel affected a doubting look.

'Well, I must say it all looks good to me, Mr Matthews. But I can't make this big a decision on my own. I'll discuss this with my business associates and get back in touch with you.'

'Fine. We hope your decision is favorable to us, Mr Jones. We welcome your business. We like to think of ourselves as partners with our depositors. Mutual investors in the future of this great territory.'

'I'll let you know,' Gabriel told him.

*   *   *

That evening at the nearby Dos Amigos saloon Gabriel looked very different from the man who had wangled bank secrets out of the junior officer. He now wore a dungaree shirt and trousers, a dark-blue bandanna at his throat and a heavy gun-belt on his hips. He was very relaxed. He knew just how much dynamite it would take to blow the bank vault some dark night, or how many guns he would need to force its opening in a daylight heist.

207

All he needed now was men.

It surprised him somewhat that the three he left at Kiowa Junction hadn't arrived here yet. If the Preacher was stalking them it seemed he would have come by now, and they would have disposed of him. Anyway, one thing was certain. Because of the probable loss of both Sweet Daddy and Cuckoo Bobo, Gabriel was short-handed. If the opportunity arose he would attempt to recruit a couple more men.

He was sitting by himself that evening. The Dos Amigos was run by Mexicans but was a large, well-appointed saloon, with real paintings on the walls, a piano player, and three saloon girls. Gabriel had already gone upstairs with the most decent-looking one, and tonight he felt like just sitting and ruminating on the riches stored at the Territorial Bank.

He ordered one planter's rye after the other, until he felt very good inside. It was then that the two men came in and sat at a table near him. Two drifters, wearing guns and looking very sure of themselves. They ordered dark ale, then the tall one poured his on to the floor when he tasted it.

'Hey, waiter! You call this horse-piss ale? I'm not paying for this stuff. Bring me a bottle of Scotch instead. And two glasses.'

'Yeah,' his shorter companion said. 'Two glasses, and hurry it up, pea-brain.'

Gabriel watched them with amusement as they laughed between themselves and spoke in low tones. When the waiter brought the bottle Gabriel called over to them.

'Hey, boys. You think you can drink that whole bottle yourselves?'

They both looked over at him hostilely. The tall one had acne on his lower face, and had wild-looking eyes. His companion was heftier, with small, pig-like eyes and a scarred right ear. They both wore sidearms: an outdated Colt and a French revolver of some kind.

'Who says we can't?' the taller one retorted.

'Bring it over here, and I'll pay for it,'

Gabriel said with a grin.

They hesitated, exchanged looks, then the tall one nodded.

'That sounds like a good enough deal to us, mister.'

When they had seated themselves with Gabriel, Gabriel continued the conversation.

'You boys from around here?'

'Are you kidding?' the tall one said. 'Is anybody from around here?'

Gabriel poured them all a drink and the piano player at the rear began playing *The Battle Hymn of the Republic*. He was stopped immediately by a cowboy with his gun out.

'Some swell joint,' the short fellow offered.

Gabriel nodded. 'I'm Simon Gabriel. I rob banks.'

Their faces changed.

'I'm Briggs,' the short one said more quietly. 'And this here is Davis. What did you say?'

'I said, I rob banks. And I was wondering if that would interest you.'

'Well, now,' Davis said. 'What makes you think we'd be interested in talk like that?'

Gabriel shrugged. 'I sized you up when you came in. You look like my kind of people. But maybe I was wrong.'

Davis looked him over. 'No. You're not wrong.'

Gabriel smiled. 'Can you really use those guns you're carrying? Or are they mostly for show?'

'Show?' The short Briggs frowned. He drew his French revolver and fired off a round. A gaslight lamp in a far corner exploded and glass scattered everywhere. All the other patrons turned to stare.

'Hey, over there!' From behind the bar. 'No shooting inside, *por favor*.'

'And Davis is better than me,' Briggs said, reholstering the gun.

'We know how to use artillery,' Davis said arrogantly. 'You may rest easy on that score.'

'OK. I'm convinced. But can you kill a man? Without hesitation?'

Briggs looked over at his partner. 'We just did,' he said.

Davis frowned heavily. 'Shut up, Briggs.'

'It's all right, boys. I don't want to know your past. I need two more men to take the Territorial Bank. Two dependable men.'

'You couldn't get two better,' Davis told him defensively.

'Good. Are you interested in splitting as much as a hundred grand?'

They both narrowed their hard eyes on him.

'A hundred grand?' Davis exclaimed, whistling between his teeth. 'They got that kind of stash there?'

'On certain days, yes,' Gabriel said. 'I've looked the place over. I've got three men coming in within a few days now. With you two, there would be six of us. Enough to do a daytime job if we hit the time lock right. I'd take the fist third of the loot, and the rest of you would split the rest. Would that sit all right with both you boys?'

They hesitated.

'Sure,' Davis finally said for both of them.

'Then you're in. If this goes well you

can ride with me. I take care of my people.'

'We got nothing better to do,' Briggs said.

'I'm leaning toward a bold daytime job,' Gabriel said after a moment. 'That would mean we'd spill some blood. Probably a couple of guards and a bank officer at most.'

The other two exchanged slow looks.

'Does that idea bother you?'

Davis ran a hand over his mouth. 'No. Not at all.'

Gabriel raised his glass. 'Then to banking success,' he said with a grin.

They followed suit.

'To success,' they said in unison.

★   ★   ★

Luther Bastian passed that whole day without running into Eddie or Big Thelma. After taking a quick look at the local saloon, and still feeling his busted rib when he moved just right, he decided it was bad judgement to push too hard to engage the enemy. One more day would make him feel a lot better, he was sure. So he would let them look for him.

But they didn't.

After Thelma's threat to Eddie about running they had a leisurely lunch at the house and discussed strategy. They were seated at a small table in a dining room off the parlor, and there was just one other guest eating with them. They waited until he had finished and left before they began talking.

'Where is he?' Eddie wondered nervously. 'This situation is making my stomach boil.'

Actually, Bastian had taken the stallion out for exercise that afternoon, after eating at a small café off the main street. He couldn't get lovely Maggie out of his head now, and he wanted very much to go see her at the clinic. But he figured that might put her in danger again, so he stayed away, as he had promised her.

'Well, it's his play, isn't it?' Thelma said too loudly. 'He's the hunter. Let him come to us. We're cash in his bank account. Remember, it's the defensive player who always has the advantage.'

'How long do we do that? Bastian wants this cat-and-mouse to be over.'

'Don't worry, it will be over. In the next day or two. He wants Gabriel, too, you know. Time is on our side.'

'If he goes after Simon he'll be pushing up daisies in the boot hill at Fort Repulse. Nobody can take Gabriel down.'

'If he goes after Gabriel, you'll already be dead,' Thelma reminded him. 'Quit thinking so far ahead.'

'You said you'd take the lead in this. What does that mean?'

'If he comes at both of us I'll draw his action to me. I can kill that yellow-stripe before he can figure out where the lead is coming from. When I draw him out, you go for him, too. But you'll be his secondary target.'

Eddie ruminated on that, and didn't like the sound of any of it. Thelma was too over-confident. She was likely to get them both killed. But he was finished with telling her that. From this point he would treat her as an adversary and keep his thoughts to himself. Because they were thoughts that Thelma definitely wouldn't want to hear.

'That sounds like it will work,' he lied. He suddenly liked making Thelma an opponent. He disliked her with a great intensity.

'You just do what I tell you,' Thelma told him, sounding more like a boss than an equal with him. He smarted under the arrogance but kept quiet about it.

They were finished. He pushed away from the table.

'Well. I might go back to the room. I'm nervous, sitting around in the open like this.'

'You're not going anywhere by yourself,' Thelma said in a threatening tone. 'Remember what I said upstairs? You don't go anywhere alone, and I wouldn't step foot in that pigsty of yours. I'm going down to the saloon and get me a couple of drinks, and you're coming along.'

Eddie remembered Thelma's quick and deadly gun.

'Thelma, I don't want a drink. We can split for an hour or two.'

'A drink will quiet your nerves,' she told him. 'You're skittish as a turkey trapped in a wire pen. Don't worry, little boy. Mama will take care of you.' She gave a hard laugh.

He frowned heavily and hated Thelma.

'A saucy manner does not go down with me, Thelma.'

Her face changed. Thelma had the cold blue stare of a killer.

'I don't care what you like and don't like,' she said in a frigid voice. 'You're playing my game now, Eddie. And you'll damn well have to like it. You don't have no say-so in this.'

He was tied up in knots inside with frustration and anger. But he kept himself under control.

'Hell. Let's go,' he said quietly.

The afternoon and evening went slowly. Bastian didn't show up at the saloon, or the boarding house, and Eddie was secretly glad. He had a plan now, and it didn't include Thelma. Thelma spent the evening reading the Kansas City newspaper and learning that there were electric lights on the streets of the nation's capital. When it came time for bed she insisted Eddie sleep in her room.

'But no funny stuff.' She grinned mockingly. 'I'm a lady, you know.'

Eddie agreed to sleep on a short sofa across the room from Thelma's bed. She exacted a solemn promise from him that he would be there at dawn.

Eddie agreed readily. He had already decided he would wait for Thelma to fall asleep, then go get his mount and ride out. She could confront the Preacher alone if that was what she wanted.

But then, as Eddie lay there on the sofa with Thelma snoring loudly across the room, he got a much bolder and better idea. If he just rode out crazy Thelma might just ride after him to kill him for deserting her. Or stay there and kill the Preacher, then bad-mouth Eddie to Gabriel. Neither scenario suited Eddie.

In the wee hours of the night therefore, with Thelma's snoring covering his movements, Eddie rose quietly, pulled his boots on, and strapped on the Iver Johnson. Then, in one of the boldest moves of his dark career, Eddie drew the gun, crept over to where Thelma lay with her back to him, and grabbed an extra pillow from her bed.

He took a deep breath in. He didn't want to fail in this. It was life or death for him. In one quick move he pressed the pillow on to Thelma's head and squeezed off a round from the revolver.

The report made a dull cracking sound in the room and Thelma's body jumped on the bed. Her hefty form then quivered all over, and afterwards there was just stillness and silence.

Eddie removed the pillow and stared down at what he had done. There was a hole in the rear of Thelma's head, and no visible blood. Her eyes were wide open, staring into her new eternity.

Eddie holstered the revolver and threw the pillow to the floor. He felt his face where she had thrown hot grease on him.

'Now who's running the show, Thelma?' he said in the semi-darkness. 'Oh, no. I won't get crossways of Gabriel. I'll tell him the Preacher killed you, and I almost got it too, defending you. He'll forgive me for not finishing the job.'

Now all that was left was to get his mount at the stable and ride out.

He felt very pleased with himself.

10

Bastian had gone to the stables to sleep earlier in the evening. His side was feeling better and he had resolved to seek out and confront Eddie and Thelma the following morning, to get this part of it over with, one way or the other. But at almost 4 a.m. his plans would no longer have any meaning.

Cottonwood Eddie went to his own room after killing Thelma, gathered up some belongings and headed down to the stables where Bastian was sleeping on a cot back near his horse, the cot having been provided by the owner. He had been asleep since before midnight when Eddie arrived.

Only a service door was open, so Eddie had to open the big doors himself. His horse was billeted at the front of the place, and he couldn't see Bastian back in the dark corner at the rear, so he had no concern about being observed. He located his saddlery and saddled up, then led the mount out through the wide doorway.

But Bastian had awakened at the sound of the doors opening, thinking it was the stable-owner. He sat up curiously. He squinted toward the opening up front and saw Eddie boarding his horse. He sat up further, drawing the Colt that he still wore.

'Hey! Who's there?'

Already mounted, Eddie turned around in shock at the sound of Bastian's voice, and in that moment Bastian saw his face clearly in the light of a full moon.

'Oh, God!' Eddie gasped out. Then he turned and spurred his mount forward.

Bastian had risen to his feet and now leveled the Colt on the figure that was disappearing fast, realizing it was Eddie. But Eddie had ducked down, giving no silhouette to shoot at. Then he was gone.

Bastian uttered an obscenity and holstered the revolver. Quickly he went to where his saddlery was stashed and began tacking up the stallion, which was very confused for a moment. He checked to make sure his long guns were returned properly to their saddle scabbards, and led the stallion out of its stall, wondering why Eddie was running alone.

Moments later he was outside the barn and mounting up. He had seen the direction Eddie had taken, but would have guessed, anyway. Eddie was heading for Fort Repulse to join up with Gabriel.

Bastian spurred the big horse into action and was soon on the road east, knowing that Eddie was somewhere up ahead and riding for his life. But Bastian knew the black stallion was the fastest horse he had ever come across, and that he would catch Eddie by dawn.

The night was a bright one, and that was to Bastian's advantage. He could even make out the dug-up hoofprints of Eddie's horse now and then in the moonlight. An hour passed, and then two. He kept the stallion at full gallop, knowing the animal could handle the extra demand on it. He could see the slather on its flanks. But he didn't let up on the pace.

Eventually light began edging on to the eastern horizon, and just as Bastian was wondering why he hadn't caught Eddie, a shot rang out from behind a stand of boulders a hundred yards ahead on his right.

Bastian reined in hard, and saw the blood on the stallion's flank. He quickly drew the Winchester 1866 from its scabbard, and jumped off the horse as another shot rang out from the rocks, tearing a hole in his black Stetson as it was knocked off his head.

Eddie had decided he couldn't outrun Bastian, so in desperation had set up an ambush: one of his favorite methods of fighting. Behind the boulders he squinted in the new light of dawn, to see if he had wounded Bastian. His mouth was dry, his heart drumming in his chest. He saw Bastian duck behind some low scrub brush and knew he wasn't hit.

'Damn, damn, damn!' he gritted out.

Bastian knelt behind the *granjeno*, rifle in hand.

'Too bad, Eddie! Now you'll have to fight like a man! Come on out in the open and take your best shot.'

'Go to hell!' Eddie cried out hysterically. A third shot followed, narrowly missing Bastian's head. Then Eddie was mounting up again. But when he spurred his mount to gallop away, he lost his cover of the rocks.

Eddie was galloping off now, over a hundred yards away. Bastian came out from behind his cover, knelt again, and settled the rifle carefully into place, his elbow on his knee, zeroing in on Eddie's back. Eddie was over a hundred yards away. Then 150 yards. At almost 200 yards, Bastian squeezed the trigger on a bobbing, receding target. The rifle cracked out sharply in the crisp morning air.

Just as he was cresting a low rise of ground, 200 yards away, that would have given him cover seconds later, Eddie was hit mid-back by the hot Winchester lead.

Eddie sat straight up in his saddle, reached to his back with his left hand, then toppled off the horse as it ran off into the distance.

It took Bastian ten minutes to corral the stallion. It had a grazing wound on its right flank, but it wasn't serious. Bastian reassured the animal, then boarded it and rode on out to Eddie.

Eddie lay on his back, still barely alive, staring into the sky. Crimson had spread on to his shirt front, where the bullet had exited. It had just missed his heart, but was a fatal shot. Bastian had won awards for long-distance shooting.

Bastian dismounted and knelt over Eddie.

'I told you to stand and fight.'

'I couldn't — beat you.'

'Incidentally, you are Cottonwood Eddie, aren't you?'

A stiff grin. 'The same.'

'Where's Thelma? Why didn't she leave with you?'

'Oh, Thelma. She'll be waiting . . . for me. In hell.'

Bastian shook his head. 'I'd thank you. But she was worth five grand.'

'She might have . . . killed you.'

Bastian just looked at him.

'Well, probably not.' Eddie coughed up some blood. 'Look. Tell Gabriel I died well.'

Bastian stood up. 'Sweet dreams, Cottonwood Eddie.'

Eddie nodded, and died.

'What the hell were you thinking?' Bastian said to the figure lying there in the dust. 'You just didn't have it for this, Eddie.'

Then he remounted the stallion and rode off without looking back.

★   ★   ★

Bastian could have headed off to Fort Repulse that morning, but he decided to return to Kiowa Junction to look at his horse's wound, and to allow himself some much-needed rest.

He arrived back in town in late morning. The owner was at the stables when Bastian returned the stallion.

'I didn't know you'd taken him out. There's another one gone, too. One of them you promised me.' The man cast

Bastian a narrow look.

'Well, I reckon you'll just have to settle for what's left here,' Bastian replied acidly. 'You see that wound in my mount's flank? I want that tended while I'm here. Is there a vet here in town?'

'No, but I can handle that.' The owner took a closer look. 'Sure, I'll get a poultice on it. He'll be ready to ride right quick.'

'Good. I'll be riding out tomorrow before you get here.'

'There will be a fee, of course.' A weak grin.

Bastian frowned at him. 'Did you ever think of going into banking?'

'Uh? I don't get it.'

'Never mind. Here. This should cover it.' He handed the fellow several coins and got a wide grin in return.

'I'll take real good care of him, mister.'

'See that you make good on that.'

'Oh, did you hear about the murder at Humphreys?'

'The woman who came here with two men?'

'That's the one. Shot dead in her bed.'

Bastian shook his head. 'Eddie, Eddie.'

'Who?'

'Just get my horse fixed up,' Bastian said as he walked away.

Bastian took a room at the boarding house himself after a quick breakfast at the same café he had visited before, then he went to bed and slept all afternoon, soundly and without disturbance. It was the best sleep he had had in several days. In late afternoon he walked to the clinic just in time to catch Maggie leaving for the day. The doctor had already gone.

Jonah was in the waiting room, reading a book Maggie had given him, and was the first to see Bastian.

'Luther!' he cried out as Bastian entered. He jumped off a chair and ran across the whitewashed room over to Bastian, hugging him around the hips and making Bastian frown in quick surprise. 'We worried about you.'

'Hey, take it easy, kid. I'm fine.' But he felt something warm surge through him with that embrace. 'I see you've been reading.'

Jonah released him. 'That was Maggie's idea. She wants to educate me. She's in the next room.'

As he said those words Maggie came through the doorway and stopped abruptly on seeing Bastian.

'Oh, dear!' she murmured softly, her eyes becoming moist.

'Hi, Maggie.' Bastian smiled. 'I hope I'm not in the way here.'

'Oh, Luther! Of course not. We've been hoping to see you again.'

'I'm leaving tomorrow for Fort Repulse. But I wanted to see you both first.'

'We heard the woman was dead,' Jonah spoke up.

Bastian nodded. 'But that wasn't me. The one called Eddie killed her. They must have had a falling-out. Anyway, Eddie ran and I followed.'

'You got him, didn't you?' Jonah said, looking up at Bastian with awe.

Bastian nodded. 'Look. Why don't I buy you both a meal at the café?'

'No, you won't,' Maggie protested. 'You'll have supper with us at my house,

Luther. I already have a pork roast ready. And we'll have privacy there.'

'How could I turn down pork roast?' Bastian smiled at her. He had never realized how good it could be to return to a woman and look upon her again.

They all walked to her house together, with Jonah asking questions about Cottonwood Eddie and Bastian diverting his attention away from the subject as much as possible. At the house, Maggie fixed their meal quickly, filling the house with good odors, while Jonah showed Bastian a couple of other books Maggie had given him to read. Throughout the meal, Maggie kept stealing looks at Bastian while he was talking to Jonah, and wishing he pursued any vocation other than the one he had chosen. The meal was delicious, and the best one Bastian had had since leaving Dallas and Brett Malory.

Afterwards they all sat on Maggie's sofa together while Jonah told stories about his grandfather and Maggie related some of her young life in Medicine Bend. Bastian surprisingly found that he liked just sitting and talking with this young woman and precocious boy. He had never had anything like this in his adult life.

At last Jonah went off to bed, and Bastian and Maggie were alone again as on that previous occasion.

They sat in complete silence for a long time, just enjoying being with each other, neither wanting to admit that fact openly. At last Maggie turned to Bastian.

'So you're still going after Gabriel?'

Bastian frowned slightly. 'I told you before. It has to be done, Maggie. And I'm the one available to do it.'

'You said you got into this because of a tragedy in your family.'

Bastian turned away from her. His long dark hair was slicked back and he had removed his gunbelts.

'I had a younger brother, Maggie. A good kid. Looked up to me and followed my lead in everything. His name was Adam. Real smart; he read books. It was just him and me, our folks had passed on, one by one. One of the last things my father told me was to take care of Adam.

I was four years older.'

'You were lucky to have him.'

He regarded her gravely. 'Yes. When it happened he was only seventeen. I left him alone one night at our cabin, to ride into town on ranch business. I knew there had been a couple of thefts in the area recently, but I figured those things happened to other folks.' He stopped, and let out a long breath.

'While I was gone, three men broke into the cabin. They tore that place up. They busted Adam up. Before they killed him.'

'Oh, Luther!'

'Don't ever tell Jonah any of this.'

'Of course not. Oh, my God, how terrible.'

'I went after them. On my own. And I killed all three. I gave every devil's son of them a chance to defend himself, too. More than they gave Adam.'

Maggie looked over at him; she was crying quietly.

'Oh, dear Luther!'

He saw the tears, and laid an arm over her shoulder.

'It's all right. Really.'

'But that's why you became a lawman. And then this. You're still trying to avenge your brother's death. On every killer out there.'

He looked into her beautiful green eyes. 'Maybe.'

'But don't you see? You couldn't predict what happened! You were attending to family business that night. Taking care of Adam in a different way. It wasn't your fault, Luther.'

'That's not what my gut tells me,' he answered her.

She dried her eyes. 'Which of the Gabriel gang actually killed that Texas Ranger in Medicine Bend?'

'We were told it was Thelma,' he said. 'Frankly, Eddie saved me a big decision. I've never shot a woman.'

'Well, then. Thelma is dead, and she did the deed. Can't you quit now? You don't have to go after Gabriel. Especially since you know, deep inside you, that this compulsion of yours will never be conquered until you decide you don't need this any more.'

He was beginning to feel uncomfortable inside. 'Maybe we better not talk about it any more, Maggie,' he told her.

'You don't even make any pretense of bringing them to justice. You're not doing this for money. You're doing it to kill killers. You'd do it for nothing.'

He rose from the sofa, and she did, too. 'Damn it, I said I'm through talking about it!' he said sharply.

She was breathless. 'Maybe I'd better get to bed.'

As she turned away he caught her arm. She turned back to him, looking distraught.

'Sorry about that.'

She nodded uncertainly.

'There's something I want to tell you. It's been in the back of my mind for months. And talking with you tonight made me think about it again.'

'What, Luther?'

'I think I'm arriving at the point where I'm getting it all worked out of me. The thing you were talking about.'

Her face changed. 'You mean it?'

'I've been thinking about quitting all this. I don't think I need to do it any more. I don't have the same anger in me now. Especially after meeting you. And Jonah.'

Her face radiated a new brightness. 'Oh, Luther!'

'But that doesn't mean I'm forgetting about Gabriel. He's part of one assignment I took on. I took it on for a good reason, Maggie. Gabriel is one of the very worst. He'll recruit new men and begin all over again. He kills like you or I would swat a fly. And in Medicine Bend he killed the wrong kind of man.'

She looked away.

'Think of what else he'll be up to, if he's allowed to go on like this. How many lives are hanging in the balance.'

Maggie looked up at him again and her face softened.

'Well. When you put it that way.'

'There's only one right way to look at it, Maggie.'

'I might not ever see you again.' Her voiced was breaking.

In that moment Bastian knew he had to see Maggie again.

'You have to trust me. I'll be back here. After the job is done.'

She felt very close to him in that moment. She came and leaned on him, and let him embrace her.

'I'll pray for that to happen,' she whispered.

★ ★ ★

In the Dos Amigos saloon in Fort Repulse Simon Gabriel had gathered his two new recruits to him again. Gabriel had expected all day that Rueda, Eddie and Thelma would be arriving from Kiowa Junction, but he waited in vain. Now, in late evening and with a couple of drinks in him, he was becoming morose about that situation.

This time the three were sitting at a table at the very rear of the big room, with a bottle of whiskey on the table between them. Gabriel swigged down the rest of a shot glass of it and stared at the table glumly.

'They're not coming,' he grunted out.

Briggs and Davis looked at each other.

'Who?' Briggs said.

Gabriel gave him a hard look. Neither of these men measured up to the likes of Pedro Rueda, or Thelma.

'Who do you think, numskull? My people!'

Briggs's face fell into straight lines. He wasn't accustomed to being insulted.

'Hey. How do we know what's in your head?'

Gabriel sighed. 'They should have been here by now. Something is wrong. And here I am, a couple hundred miles away. No way of knowing if they're dead or alive. But I do know. He showed up in Kiowa Junction, and he killed them.'

'Who killed them?' Davis spoke up this time.

Gabriel met his enquiring look. 'There's this bounty hunter.'

'Oh,' the hefty Briggs said. 'One of them dung heaps.'

'This one is different,' Gabriel went

on. 'I heard a couple stories about him. Used to wear a badge. But he got tired of arresting people, I guess. He took the badge off and went to hunting men for money. He never takes a man in. Word is, he's killed over a dozen men with dodgers on them.'

Davis whistled between his teeth. 'So. Is he good?'

'If he killed my boy Daddy, he's very dangerous,' Gabriel said, more to himself than to them.

'Well, if he's in Kiowa Junction, he's no problem to us,' Briggs offered. 'Anyway, Davis here can beat any bounty hunter.'

'Really?' Gabriel said in a sour tone. 'Draw on me, Davis.'

'What?'

'I said, draw on me. Let's see how fast you are.'

'This is crazy, Gabriel. You'll see when the time comes. In the bank.'

'We might not make it to the bank,' Gabriel said. He rose from his chair. 'Go ahead. Draw.'

Davis hesitated, then rose too, facing

him across the table. A couple of patrons near by stopped drinking to watch the action. Davis and Gabriel were now face to face, hands over guns. Suddenly Davis went for his revolver, and he was fast. But by the time he had cleared leather Gabriel's Army Colt was leveled at his heart.

Davis looked at the muzzle of the other gun in shock.

Briggs muttered something under his breath, eyes wide.

Gabriel holstered the Colt and sat back down.

'My boy Sweet Daddy was faster than that. And he's six feet under at Medicine Bend now.'

Davis sat back down, subdued. 'I see what you mean.'

'This guy is called the Preacher. Something about the way he dresses. The point is, he didn't stop at Medicine Bend, where he found Daddy and Bobo. He rode on to Kiowa Junction to find my other people, it looks like. If they're all dead, he'll come here. He's going after my whole gang, including me.'

'Why?' Briggs wondered.

'I can think of only one reason. We killed a meddlesome Texas Ranger in Medicine Bend. That was probably a mistake. The Rangers never forget. They might have hired this Preacher to hunt us all down. And I'll be next.'

'Let him come,' Briggs said. 'If he finds you, we'll stand with you. It will be three against him. And I just saw you draw. There's no way he can beat you.'

Gabriel poured another glass of whiskey. 'That's what I've been telling myself. But he's done pretty damn well so far. Anyway, I don't want to stick around here waiting for him to make his try. So we'll have to hit the bank with what we've got right here at this table. And we don't have enough for a day job. Has either of you ever handled explosives?'

'I did demolition work at a quarry in Abilene,' Davis said.

'Good. I want you to figure what it will take to blow that safe. We'll make a second visit together, give you a feel for the place. I want to take it in the next couple of days. At night.'

Davis nodded. 'I can handle that.'

'Sure,' Briggs said. 'We're in.'

'Meet me at the hotel tomorrow afternoon,' Gabriel told them. 'I'll take both of you with me. Clean yourselves up, and leave the artillery off.'

'We can't wear our guns?' Briggs frowned.

'They think I'm a respectable business-man. If I can pass you two off as associates we can get another look at their safe. Up close.'

'That's all I'll need.' Davis grinned.

'Then I'll see you tomorrow.'

'We'll be there,' Briggs said eagerly.

Gabriel took a long swallow of whis-key from his glass. He had always been good at changing plans quickly when the need arose. They would help them-selves to the cash in the bank's vault, and he would be on his way before the Preacher got there. Then Gabriel would ride north to Missouri, where the bounty hunter would never think to look for him.

It would all work out after all.

11

It was a long, hard ride to Fort Repulse.
When Bastian arrived there, late in the
day, he took a room at a hotel, fell into
bed and slept for almost twelve hours.
When he awoke the next morning, unknown
to him, Simon Gabriel was planning to
rob the Territorial Bank that very night.

Davis had purchased enough dynamite to blow the safe, and had had a
good look at the vault the previous day,
with Gabriel.

Everything was in order. Gabriel would
ride out of town that same night with his
new partners in crime, hoping that the
Preacher would not arrive in time for a
confrontation. Not that Gabriel really
feared the bounty hunter, but he didn't
want any extraneous events to ruin his
plans for that night, or the future. Things
could go unexpectedly wrong in a face-
down, and he didn't want even a slight

risk of big trouble.

In early morning, though, Bastian checked at the other two hotels in town, and found out that Gabriel was registered at one of them from a description given him by the desk clerk. He also learned that Gabriel left a bit earlier with two other men, and he realized Gabriel had new recruits. His stallion stabled, he walked down to the nearest saloon to the hotel, figuring Gabriel might be there. It was the Dos Amigos. Gabriel wasn't there, nor were Davis or Briggs. But the bartender confirmed they had been.

Bastian ordered a beer and sat at a table not far from the front entrance, to think things over. He hadn't wanted the chance of facing down more than Gabriel in a confrontation. That raised the odds against him. Gabriel himself was good enough with a gun to kill Bastian.

He had been sitting there for just ten minutes when a rather tall man walked into the saloon wearing a badge. He paused at the door, took a look at Bastian, and walked right over to him.

'You're the Preacher, aren't you?'

He was a strapping, middle-aged man, lean and fit-looking, wearing a Peacemaker on his hip. He had a bony face with lines put there by years of weather and hardship.

Bastian sighed. 'I'm Luther Bastian, yes.'

'I seen you once in Kansas. I'm Padgett. US deputy marshal.'

Bastian nodded. 'Am I under arrest?'

Padgett sat down at the table and leaned toward him.

'Don't play games with me, Bastian. You don't show up unless there's money to be made. You know Simon Gabriel is here, don't you?'

Bastian held his hard gaze. 'What if I do?'

'This is what. I'm here to arrest Gabriel. We got hard evidence he murdered a shotgun rider in a stage hold-up last year not far from here. I'm just waiting till I find him alone, without them two cronies. He shares a two-bed room with them. And I don't want any interference from the likes of you. I hope you understand me.'

'I think I'm getting it, Marshal.'

'The US government arrests outlaws, Bastian, a concept you're not familiar with. You should ride on out. You have no business to conduct here.'

Bastian thought about that. Maybe it wasn't such a bad thing that Padgett had showed up. Brett Mallory couldn't blame him if he was warned off by the law. If Gabriel stood trial he would hang by the neck until dead, and Bastian could begin putting all this behind him.

'Look, I won't give you any trouble, Marshal.' All the way there on that long trail he had been thinking about what Maggie had said to him. 'I'd decided not to collect the bounty on him, anyway.'

Padgett regarded him curiously. 'A bounty hunter rides all the way here to kill a man, and doesn't want the reward money? Then can you tell me why you came at all?'

'You probably haven't heard this yet.

His people killed a Texas Ranger.'

Padgett's lean face creased in a heavier frown. 'Hmm. That's bad.'

'Brett Mallory sent me to take him down,' Bastian said. 'I've already met up with some of his gang. They won't be joining him here.'

Padgett sat back on his seat. 'I reckon I should thank you. But that don't change things.'

Bastian leaned forward, too. 'I'm sure they murdered that Ranger without giving it a second thought. It would be the same with you.'

'I know Gabriel isn't afraid of shooting lawmen,' Padgett responded. 'But that makes no difference to me. Gabriel has to stand trial for the world to see what kind of animal he is.'

'I suspect most of the world around here already knows,' Bastian offered. 'But here's the thing. Gabriel is good. Very good. Even if you find him by himself, he's likely to kill you. Sorry to be so blunt about it, but that's the truth of it.'

'I might not be as good as him. Or

you. But I've survived face-downs with some pretty dangerous fellows, Bastian. And I do my duty. Wherever it takes me.'

'I could be there. With you. When you make the arrest.'

Padgett laughed easily. 'I want him alive, Bastian. I'm not sure you know how to do that. Anyway, how would it look if I let a bounty man help me make an arrest? I think I'll pass on that.'

Bastian raised his brows. 'Well. I guess there's nothing left for me but to keep out of your way.'

'I think that's best.'

*   *   *

Bastian left Padgett sitting there quietly, lost in his own thoughts. Bastian returned to his hotel and had a light lunch in the dining room there, reflecting on what had just happened. Despite what the marshal might want, Bastian couldn't just ride out. He wouldn't know whether Gabriel's arrest had been successful. If it wasn't, Bastian's job was not over.

249

After his meal was finished, he decided to return to the saloon and ask Padgett how to keep in touch with him through the next forty-eight hours or so. It seemed like a reasonable request.

In the meantime Padgett had left the saloon, gone to eat at a nearby restaurant, and then returned to the Dos Amigos, entering warily in case Gabriel had brought his men there. There were a number of patrons present, but not Gabriel or his men. The saloon's piano player was playing a lively tune, and a saloon girl was busy seducing a cowboy at the long bar.

The marshal decided to stay a while and hope Gabriel came in alone. He ordered another dark ale and sat quietly up near the front entrance.

Less than a half-hour later Simon Gabriel walked in with Davis and Briggs right behind him.

Padgett saw them immediately, and lowered his head, not wanting to make eye contact, wishing suddenly he had taken his badge off. It was his duty, he knew, if he followed the manual, to confront them, regardless of their numbers. But Padgett had survived so long because he didn't follow unreasonable rules. He swigged his ale and resolved to leave without confronting Gabriel.

The threesome were at the bar, ordering drinks in preparation to finding a table, when Briggs looked toward the front of the place and spotted Padgett's badge.

'Oh-oh. Look what we have here.'

Gabriel and Davis followed his gaze, and saw the marshal.

'Well, well,' Gabriel said softly.

'Good God! A US marshal,' Davis muttered. 'Let's get out of here.'

'No, no,' Gabriel said. 'The good marshal might be here watching us. I don't want the law watching us, with our big plans.'

'What can we do about it?' Briggs whispered.

'The same thing I did in Medicine Bend,' Gabriel replied in a hard voice. 'When a Texas Ranger came to look us over. We got rid of him.'

Davis looked over at him. 'You mean . . . ?'

'Exactly.'

'But there's this whole room of witnesses,' Davis protested.

'After he's dead who will they report this to? Anyway, we'll get him to draw. That's all it takes.'

Briggs licked suddenly dry lips. He had only signed on to rob a bank. Across the room Padgett threw some coins down on his table and rose to his feet.

'You're not thinking of leaving, are you, Marshal?' Gabriel asked in a hard, arrogant voice. Padgett sighed and turned to them.

'So you spotted me. Well, that's just as well, Gabriel. Because I'm placing you under arrest.' He made no move for his gun.

Gabriel grinned. 'On what charge, Marshal? I been minding my business here in town. You just here to harass ordinary citizens?'

'Yeah,' Briggs blustered. 'What's going on here?'

The piano went silent at the rear of the room. Conversations at tables ceased abruptly. The Latina saloon girl turned from the cowboy at the bar and the Mexican bartender stood transfixed.

'Let's not have any trouble here, *amigos*,' he said nervously.

'Shut up,' Gabriel told him. He turned to Davis. 'Why don't you get that table over there for us?'

Davis nodded and walked over to a table about fifteen feet away. Briggs stood near Gabriel; the three now had Padgett flanked.

'So. That's the way it is,' Padgett said quietly to Gabriel.

'That's the way it is, Marshal. I've never been arrested and won't allow you to tarnish that record. You're talking to an innocent man here.'

'Well, if you'll come with me we can discuss that at the proper place,' Padgett said. His stomach had tightened up in knots, because he understood that this had to end in a shoot-out. With Gabriel, there was no other way.

'I can't hear you when you talk like that, Marshal.' Gabriel grinned confidently. 'If you want to take me in, you better reach for iron. And I invite everybody in this room to take note that this man is the aggressor in this.'

'I'm the law, Gabriel,' the tall Padgett said stiffly. 'And you've been the aggressor for some time now. I'll ask you to disarm yourself. You and your friends here.'

It was a brave thing to say, but suicidal. Three customers rose and left through a rear door. The girl at the bar sucked her breath in and quit breathing.

'Like hell,' Gabriel growled. 'It's your move, Marshal.'

All sound ceased in the big room. For a moment it looked like a still daguerreotype photograph. Padgett looked at the three men poised to draw on him, and took a deep breath in.

Then the big swinging doors just in back of him swung open and Luther Bastian walked into the room, his spurs making metallic music in the silence.

He stopped beside Padgett, taking in the situation. Looking tall, dark and dangerous, with the altered Peacemaker boldly announcing its presence on his belly.

Gabriel distinctly uttered a low profanity.

'Jesus!' Briggs muttered, beside him.

'Well,' Bastian said to the room. 'What have we here, Marshal? A little game of three-to-one developing?'

Padgett looked over at him with an inward sigh of relief.

'You don't have to get into this, Bastian,' he said quietly.

'I do a lot of things I don't have to do,' Bastian replied. He let his gaze fall on Gabriel. 'So you're Simon Gabriel.'

Gabriel had regained his composure. 'So you're the Preacher. It looks like fate has thrown us together at last.'

'I've been looking forward to the meeting,' Bastian told him.

Gabriel grunted. 'You killed them, didn't you?'

'Your people? They had bounties on their heads.'

'If it's money you want I can give you plenty. Just leave quietly and let us deal with the marshal.'

'What's the matter, Gabriel? Don't like it that the odds have been whittled down some?'

Another patron rose quickly and hurried past Padgett and Bastian to the front doors. The girl at the bar was trying to breathe, her chest heaving. Drinkers sat wide-eyed around the room, waiting.

'It don't make any difference to me, Preacher. You're not dealing with Cottonwood Eddie now. I'm not standing for arrest, and neither of you is leaving here.'

The tension was palpable in the room. Nobody moved. Nobody breathed.

'Then go for your iron,' Bastian responded.

In the next few seconds an explosive roar of gunfire erupted in that room that deafened eardrums and shook bottles on shelves.

Gabriel's Colt was the first out, splitting the silence like a cleaver, and Bastian's Peacemaker banged out a half-second later. Gabriel's lead hit Bastian in the high left shoulder and staggered him backwards. But he had already returned fire, and the hot slug had hit Gabriel midchest, smashing through his breastbone and tearing a hole in his heart before exiting past a posterior rib. Gabriel went flying off his feet, an expression of utter disbelief on his heavy, scarred face.

The marshal's gun had also boomed out, at the same moment as Davis's, as they fired at each other. Davis's shot slammed into Padgett's low chest and broke ribs, sending him stumbling against the front wall of the room. Padgett's lead struck Davis just above the groin in the belly and he yelled loudly, going down doubled over.

Bastian's Colt had fired off a second time, and hit Davis again as Davis tried to rise to fire, and Davis stared at the ceiling unseeing. Briggs got a shot in, too, hitting Padgett a second time, in the right arm, as Padgett leaned, stunned, against the wall.

Then Bastian's Colt blasted out yet

again, as he fanned the hammer, and Briggs was slugged in the forehead, whip-lashing his head, making him run wildly past a table and take it down with him as he crashed to the floor.

Seven seconds had elapsed.

Gunsmoke was so thick in the air it clogged the nostrils and gave an iron taste on the tongue, even occluding vision for a few moments. At the bar the saloon girl made a choking sound in her throat and fainted, collapsing to the floor. The barkeep fell back on to his shelves and knocked a bottle down.

'Good Jesus!' The oath was uttered in a hushed voice by a patron at the rear.

Bastian still stood, looking very dangerous. He twirled the Peacemaker three times forward in a deft movement, then let it slide backward into its holster.

'Damn!' muttered another patron.

Bastian went over to where Gabriel lay with a hole in his chest. He was very dead. Davis was also dead, as was Briggs.

Bastian turned from them and walked over to Padgett, who was sitting on the floor now, holding his side with his shot arm. Bastian examined his wounds, and nodded.

'You'll be all right, Marshal.' His own in his shoulder now ached badly. He made a face when he stood up and turned to the bartender.

'Get a medic in here, barkeep. And maybe an undertaker.'

He helped Padgett to his feet and got him seated on a chair. The bartender revived his girl and got her up; she left the room in a daze. Then the bartender and another man left for help. Bastian looked at his shoulder and saw a lot of blood on his shirt and coat there. But the lead hadn't hit bone. He had been lucky again.

Drinkers wanted to congratulate Bastian and buy him drinks, but he waved them off, watching over Padgett until he was taken away on a stretcher. Bastian accompanied him in a horse-drawn ambulance to a nearby clinic; by mid-afternoon he had been bandaged up and his arm put in a sling. The tape was finally taken off his fractured rib. He felt good.

But he knew now that his bounty-hunting days were finished. His career had ended with a bang, and that was probably appropriate, he figured.

At last he could look for a way to turn his life around, actually make something of it.

★　★　★

The next day Bastian felt like a different man. He went to a local store and bought work clothes to replace the black outfit he had worn for so long, since his brother's death. He also purchased a rawhide vest and a dark-brown Stetson. He even discarded the shoulder holster with its Meriden revolver, and stashed it in a saddle-bag with his Webley. The Peace-maker was retained for defense.

Before he left town he visited Padgett at the clinic. The marshal was recovering nicely and would live to serve again.

'I was stupidly stubborn, Bastian,' he

said from his bed. 'I can't tell you the relief I felt when you walked in there. You saved my life. I won't ever forget it.'

'I'm glad I decided to go find you again,' Bastian told him.

'How's your shoulder?'

'It will heal fast. I'm riding out, Marshal. I just wanted to wish you the best.'

'I see you got a different look now. Is that significant?'

'I'm quitting this,' Bastian said. 'I don't need it any more.'

'What will you do?'

Bastian shrugged. 'We'll see.'

'Well, good luck to you. You deserve it.'

A short time later Bastian was riding out of town. He was heading for Texas. But he had a stop to make in Kiowa Junction first.

Because of the shoulder wound Bastian took two days to get there. The shoulder ached badly when he arrived back at Kiowa Junction in late afternoon. The clinic was still open, so he stopped there to get something for the pain. And to see Maggie and Jonah.

Jonah was in the waiting room again, by himself, as all patients had already been treated for the day, and had left. Jonah looked up casually from an arithmetic book and didn't recognize Bastian at first look. Then his eyes widened, and a big smile took over his face.

'Luther!' he yelled at the top of his lungs. In another moment he was running to Bastian and hugging him tightly, as if not to lose him again. Bastian grimaced in pain when the arm sling was jostled.

'How've you been, boy?' he asked in a quiet, warm voice.

'You got him, didn't you? You killed Gabriel?'

'That's right.'

'Oh! You're shot.'

'It's all right, Jonah. It's good to see you again.'

At that moment the doctor emerged from the examination room and stopped to stare at him.

'Good Lord! Luther Bastian.'

'Hi, Doc. I thought you might have something to make this feel better.'

'Of course we do. I'll get you some laudanum. I'll tell Maggie you're here.'

The doctor disappeared inside the other room, leaving Jonah still standing close to Bastian, holding Bastian's good hand. Then Maggie appeared in the doorway, eyes wide, face flushed with excitement.

'You did it! You're back!' Her eyes were tearing up. She went to him and embraced him even more tightly than Jonah had. Bastian lasted through the pain. 'I'm so glad, Luther. I don't know how I got through it.'

Bastian's face went sober at those remarks. Nobody had cared that much about his well-being since his brother died on that fateful night.

'Maggie. I'm heading out for west Texas. There's a piece of ranch land out that way, right on the Rio Grande. I've decided to buy it and put a cabin on it. Buy a small herd and become a rancher. It beats what I've been doing.'

263

'Why, that sounds wonderful, Luther. I see you've already bought the clothes for it. You look — different, better.'

'I want you and Jonah to go with me,' Bastian said.

The doctor had just come through the door with a bottle. He heard the offer, and again stopped abruptly where he was, to hear Maggie's response.

'Oh, my gosh!' Jonah was yelling out. 'When do we leave?'

But Maggie's face had gone somber. She released Bastian and looked away.

'I can't do that, Luther. The doctor needs me here. I can't just abandon him and his practice. I'm sorry, but I can't.'

The doctor put the bottle down, came over and took Maggie by the shoulders.

'Now you listen to me, young lady. How many times have I told you to leave Kiowa Junction and find a life for yourself? Anyway, I'll be retiring one day soon, and you'd be out of a job. Do you want to go with him?'

Maggie looked into Bastian's dark-brown eyes.

'Very much,' she admitted.

Bastian and Jonah both grinned at her.

'Well, then. I'm sorry, Maggie, but you're fired. You're just not worth the big salary I pay you.' Maggie turned to him with damp eyes.

'Thanks, Doctor.' She hugged him to her for a moment, then let her gaze fall back on Bastian. 'Yes, we'll go. This is what I've wanted ever since I first saw you.'

'Great!' Jonah yelled out again. 'I'm going to be a rancher.'

Not long after that Bastian got his laudanum, and the doctor said his good-byes to Maggie, and Jonah was sent outside to get the stallion ready for the stables. Bastian and Maggie were alone.

'This wouldn't have worked without you, Maggie,' he said. 'And Jonah.'

She put her arm around him. 'We'll make a life together,' she said. 'A real life.'

'When we get there I'll make you an honest woman.'

She laughed. 'I wouldn't have it any other way.'

'I'll be leaving at dawn tomorrow,' he said. 'Will you be ready?'

Her answer was exactly what he wanted to hear.

'I've been ready ever since you hugged me to you that night Rueda tried to kill you,' she said.

Bastian let a long breath out. The Preacher was gone, never to return. And at that moment in his eternity, his future looked brighter than he could ever have imagined.

We do hope that you have enjoyed reading this large print book.

Did you know that all of our titles are available for purchase?

We publish a wide range of high quality large print books including:
Romances, Mysteries, Classics
General Fiction
Non Fiction and Westerns

Special interest titles available in large print are:
The Little Oxford Dictionary
Music Book, Song Book
Hymn Book, Service Book

Also available from us courtesy of Oxford University Press:
Young Readers' Dictionary
(large print edition)
Young Readers' Thesaurus
(large print edition)

For further information or a free brochure, please contact us at:
Ulverscroft Large Print Books Ltd.,
The Green, Bradgate Road, Anstey,
Leicester, LE7 7FU, England.
Tel: (00 44) **0116 236 4325**
Fax: (00 44) **0116 234 0205**

Other titles in the
Linford Western Library:

GARRETT'S TRAIL
TO JUSTICE

Terrell L. Bowers

Dayton Garrett is a roving trouble-shooter, taking on jobs from town-taming to bringing down a counterfeiting ring. Charged with searching for a missing child, he fetches up in Shilo, where his attorney brother Knute provides him with helpful information — and requests a favour in return. Alyson Walsh has been convicted of murder in a kangaroo court, and faces the noose in two days' time. Knute wants her broken out of jail while he endeavours to get her a fair trial — and Dayton is just the man for the job . . .

QUINCY'S QUEST

Jay Clanton

Down on his luck, Martin Quincy falls in with crooked company, and agrees to participate in a train robbery. The hold-up is successful, netting Quincy over three thousand dollars. But later he's shocked to discover that one of the other thieves shot a woman in front of her child — and when he castigates them, they beat him, steal his money, and leave him for dead in the desert. Quincy, however, is made of stern stuff — and swears to track them down and kill every one of them . . .

RAWHIDE EXPRESS

Jake Douglas

Hardluck Lacy, they call him. The nickname's fitting for a man who gets three years in the penitentiary after defending himself in a fist-fight which leaves his opponent dead. And the moniker follows him to his old stamping ground, where old friends have now become new enemies. But years in prison have hardened him, and now he's ready for anything. Or so he hopes . . .

SUNDOWN OVER THE SIERRAS

Dale Graham

When Marshal Chase Farlow responds to a break-in at Macy's gun shop, he has no inkling of the ignominy it will unleash. His unfortunate shooting of the culprit forces him to leave town in disgrace. It matters not that the injury is superficial, and Farlow was only doing his duty — the boy in question is Mayor Abner Stanton's son, and the highly principled lawman has become a thorn in Stanton's side. Can Farlow somehow resurrect his tarnished reputation?

THE BOUNTY HUNTER

Billy Hall

Bounty hunter Orrin Reed never goes after a man who doesn't deserve to die or be put away, never targets anyone about whom there is any question of guilt, never pursues a person whose crime could possibly have been justified. After Nate Neidermeyer slips through his fingers, Orrin trails him into the wilderness and takes him prisoner. But the river rages high and wild, friends of Nate are riding to his rescue, and the scattered forest provides inadequate cover. Can Orrin escape these deadly straits, or is he doomed?